Dreams of Love

Three P's in a Pod

E.K. Cooper

iUniverse, Inc.
Bloomington

Dreams of Love
Threee P's in a Pod

iUniverse books may be ordered through booksellers or by contacting:

iUniverse
1663 Liberty Drive
Bloomington, IN 47403
www.iuniverse.com
1-800-Authors (1-800-288-4677)

ISBN: 978-1-4620-6902-6 (sc)
ISBN: 978-1-4620-6900-2 (e)
ISBN: 978-1-4620-6901-9 (dj)

Library of Congress Control Number: 2011961238

Printed in the United States of America
iUniverse rev. date: 12/7/2011

THIS BOOK IS DEDICATED TO MY MOTHER

JOAN C. RILEY-COOPER
August 31, 1938 – April 12, 2002

I dedicate this book to the most magnificent woman I have ever known, my mother, whose death inspired me to start putting my thoughts in writing and to compile my previous writings into one or several things.

I have been writing poetry since I was in elementary school. Writing poems, speeches, and opening and closing remarks for school plays had become somewhat of a hobby over the years. However, I never thought or took the time to put the writings all together. Devastated after my mom's sudden death, my inner thoughts merged with my creative writing and collectively went down on paper.

I picked up my pen about thirty days after her death and have not put it down since. It was approximately four years later that I realized I had found a way to cope with my loss. Each personal poem, greeting card, or short story I write reminds me of my inspiration and how blessed I am to have had a mother like mine. Completing this book is a major accomplishment and a wonderful way to honor the memory of my rock, the matriarch of my family, my mother.

A Daughter's Love

Although we are apart
You're always in my heart
And if grief makes me write
Then this I will not fight
I'll always want you proud of me
Even if you're not here to see
For my love for you will forever last
Even until the minute I pass

Written by E. K.
1/09

Acknowledgments

***My humble gratitude to the Creator of the Universe
for all things***

Gratitude and love to my only brother, James E. Cooper, the only person who really understood and stuck very close to me after our mother's death. We cried many tears through my first four years of consistent writing; every poem I wrote was about our mother. He was the first person to e-mail my poetry to family members. I was not pleased in the beginning; he was sharing my personal feelings about our mother with others. I eventually got over it and started compiling all of my poetry into one book. Then came the ten short love stories. I realized completing this book would be a wonderful honor and a great tribute to our mother's memory.

Special thanks and love to my daughter-in-law Ahavia, who read every story as it was finished. She gave me the encouragement to continue writing and complete this book.

Special thanks and respect to my friend and co-worker Sabrina, who critiqued my stories and gave me feedback from the perspective of a mother of a teenage daughter.

Extra special thanks to one of my girls, Tzuriyah, who was the only young person out of five, who made the time between school and her high school graduation preparations, to read my book.

It was an even better feeling when she informed me that she had gotten the message and really enjoyed the book.

Love and thanks to my four sons and other two daughters-in-law; three grandsons, Lifnaiyah, Shamayah, and Khaziel; four beautiful granddaughters, Zimriyah Kai, Nakaliah, Yaviayl and Yaphiah; and to my only sister-in-law, Hilton Cooper. They all continuously inspired me and gave me the confidence and support to complete this book and share my stories.

I truly love you all.

Contents

Acknowledgments   ix

Introduction   xiii

Three Peas in a Pod   xv

1.   A Dream of Love (Precious, a P in the Pod)   1

2.   Princess (A P in a New Pod)   6

3.   Patrick and Penene (Two P's That Made the Pod)   15

4.   An Afternoon of Intimacy (A P in a Pod)   23

6.   Did Pretty Meet Her Match? (A P in the Pod) Part One   34

7.   Did Pretty Meet Her Match? (A P in a Pod) Part Two   45

8.   Tricks of Love (A P in a Pod) Part One   56

9.   Tricks of Love … This Is Not a Dream Part Two   65

10. Precious's Confession and Pretty's Honeymoon
(Two Ps in a Pod)   79

Introduction

Dreams of Love: Three *P's in the Pod* is ten short love stories about the lives and the family of three sisters whose names all begin with the letter P. The stories are based on the personal values that Princess, Pretty, and Precious were taught by their parents. In growing up, the sisters made a pact to save their virginity for their husbands. If a man was willing to stick around to marry them, then he was worthy to receive their treasure. They were taught that their treasure was something special; and it was one thing that they had control over, besides their reputations.

The short stories reflect everyday issues and thoughts of intimacy that young women experience while trying to uphold their values. The fictional reflections are based on real situations that many young women experience and are too embarrassed to speak about, oftentimes. Some situations become a struggle, especially when feelings of lust, intimacy, and confusion begin to manifest.

Dreams of Love is centered on Precious, the youngest sister, who is constantly seeking love ... sensual, romantic, storybook love. In her quest for love, she dreams and puts her intimate thoughts on paper. In her dreams it is as if she has loved before, somewhere, somehow. Every time Precious closes her eyes, she sees and feels love. Amazingly, her poetic stories of love seem to affect everyone around her. Ironically, everyone around her seems to find love as she continues her search. The question is, will Precious ever really find the love that she so desperately desires?

As you explore the three Ps in a pod and Precious's dreams of love, you will find that you can relate to a story or two. You'll find them funny, hot, sensuous, intimate, romantic, and sometimes very real … so real you may find yourself having a dream.

Three Peas in a Pod

Three Ps in a pod, what will they do
Green as the shell they all cling to

Now Princess, the eldest, will get to experience it first
While Pretty is hastily trying to quench her sexual thirst

And poor naïve Precious, running around gleaming
Always looking for true love and constantly dreaming

That pact they made is so hard to keep
With their lustful desires that burn so deep

But their feelings are real and their movements are bold
And nothing stands firmer than the values they hold

1. A Dream of Love
(Precious, a P in the Pod)

Just as any other warm summer morning, I awoke a bit early to the sound of birds singing their love songs and the sun shining ever so brightly through my bedroom window. Instead of getting out of bed, I turned sideways, facing the window, just to feel the warm sun on my cheeks. The sound of the birds chirping was so sweet that I closed my eyes just to try to understand the songs they were singing back and forth. It sounded like a series of love songs, and I was so eager to know the words. It was a heavenly sound to my ears. As I opened my eyes for a moment and gazed out at the trees, suddenly a colorful bird flew close by and landed on a branch full of leaves near my window; there the sun just glistened on the bird, a beautiful rainbow of colors. In that instant the songs became so loud that I drifted off into a deep sleep.

It was a warm day in May, and I found myself sitting outside on the grass, listening to my two older sisters talking, as usual, about men. My eldest sister, Princess, was planning her wedding, which was scheduled for August of the next year. All she spoke of was her upcoming wedding and her honeymoon. She and her future husband had planned to go to some fancy honeymoon suite in Hawaii.

Princess talked and talked about her honeymoon, but she had no clue whatsoever what any kind of intimacy with a man meant.

Our parents had given us the names Princess, Pretty, and Precious, the three Ps, and they had an explanation for all three names. It was "Future Princess," "Simply Pretty," and "My Precious." Every one of us fit our names to a tee. Princess had a royal attitude and a regal look. She always dressed like royalty; she even walked like a future queen. Believe it, the man in her life had to treat her like one, and she had found him. Ironically, his name was King Malech, and yes, we teased her often; we always had a good laugh. Princess had always planned to marry a man that had money, a good job, etc. … she never wanted to want for anything. I use to think her name was a curse only because it suited her so well.

Now Pretty was different; she was a little rough and tough. No one messed with her growing up. She would fool the average man because she was so pretty, yet so strong willed and strong bodied. As for me, "My Precious," I was just that … precious. I was the baby, so everyone held me a bit closer; they were overprotective and, yes, they spoiled me. I attracted mates that would be very protective of me; if they weren't they wouldn't really appeal to me much. As time passed I've come to realize we all really live up to our names.

As my sisters' conversation about men and love intensified, I was just daydreaming, letting the warm sun hit my face, laughing at them quietly. Out of the three of us, I thought I knew the most when it came to intimate issues only because I read, wrote, and dreamed more about it. Love and intimacy were always on my mind in one way or another. Princess spoke only about what a man could buy or do for her and how she would look. Pretty just didn't want a wimp or a soft man. She wanted someone challenging, firm, and often (get my drift?). She just wanted someone that could really handle her. I don't think love was really an issue for her.

We sisters did a lot of talking. We were normally curious about sex, especially when we started experiencing lustful and unexplainable urges, even though we were raised very old-fashioned. We still managed to make a vow to save ourselves for marriage. One thing we knew from our parents: our bodies were sacred and were all we really had to call our own. A man had to be worthy and committed to receive our goodies. We all managed to stick to our vow, probably because we lived in the boondocks, away from the masses. I believe that was our parents' plan all along. However, living in the sub-suburbs really wasn't so bad; we always had neighbors, and we did have plenty of friends, boys and girls. We thought our growing up was very normal.

Princess was twenty-five years old and had finished college last August, and she worked for the same bank for the past two years. She was scheduled for a promotion to senior executive financial officer any day. Her fiancé, King, no doubt was a vice president for another bank; they were a match made in heaven.

Pretty was twenty-three and was a physical education instructor in a junior high school. She was somewhat dainty and very pretty, but sometimes if you heard her speak, she would shock you. She was so bold and boisterous about whatever she wanted to do or say. She wasn't afraid of saying much of anything, either.

Now I, Precious, on the other hand, was so elegantly homely and fragile, not enough to break into pieces, but lovingly precious. I was the twenty-one-year-old elementary school teacher, always doing something with the children in school and in our community.

I am that sister that's always looking for true love, an intimate knight in shining armor, loving yet gentle and full of romance and passion. I am the dreamer looking for a fairy-tale lover, I presumed. For some reason I didn't really believe or think one really existed, especially according to my sisters and our girlfriends. I had decided to create my own lover most of the time, with a little bit of everything from all the female doubters' imaginations, and yes, my imagination was the largest.

All of a sudden, Princess and Pretty were all over me, laughing. "Please don't tell us you're dreaming about your lover again; girl, snap out of it!".

I told them both to get off of me; they were both crazy and jealous, *that's all.* "*Neither one of you has an idea of what it would or should be like.*"

"*Oh, please, describe it to us,*" *they said. I threw up my hands, waving them off and said,* "*You're not even ready, believe me.*"

Princess then said, "*Come on, Precious, tell me. I'm getting married soon; I need to know something and you have some good stories to tell. I need to hear one right about now. I want to make sure I have some kind of idea about something.*"

With a lustful look on her face, Pretty then said, "*You know all he has to be is …*"

"*Don't say it,*" *said Princess.* "*Your mind is so vulgar. I don't think you will ever make love,*" *she said,* "*but I, on the other hand, want to learn something.*"

"*You act like Precious knows how to make love; she has never had any in her life,*" *said Pretty.*

"*No, she hasn't, but admit it … when you hear her stories she can really make you believe she has.*"

Pretty then yelled, "*Hey, Precious, did you get some before us in the class closet or something?*" *She laughed really hard.*

"*Be quiet, Pretty,*" *I yelled back.* "*Leave me alone. That's why you're going to be a virgin forever.*"

"*Hey, don't say that; I want to be married before I'm thirty,*" *said Pretty.*

Princess grabbed my arm. "*Come on, Precious, come on, tell me a love story, I'm serious … tell us one.*" *Princess slowly laid back on the grass, pulling my arm.*

I just laid on my back and closed my eyes. I then said, "*Okay, but you'd better not laugh this time. I mean it, or I'll never tell you another story.*"

Pretty started laughing. "*She won't need to hear any more stories; soon she'll have her own stories to tell.*"

"*Pretty, relax, listen, and learn something, would you?*" *said Princess.*

Then I started smiling with my eyes closed, and in a soft sweet voice I said, "*Hi, honey, are you on your way home? I have everything waiting for you. I miss you. I can't stop thinking and yearning for you. I'm just thinking about your moist and warm observer seriously exploring my hidden treasures and my valuable tenders, sending me on a safe and exciting journey to an outer place, a place where only I go, only when you choose to send me there …*

"*Your strong, manly presence feeling like a snug blanket around me, covering me, protecting me like a mother protecting her nest … oh baby, I feel your sweet and heated essence, slowly entering my spiritual realm, slowly and gently driving me insane. All of this with a tenderness and confidence of a skilled sculptor, creating and molding a masterpiece, one that moves only in the directions that you choose … when you choose … then fireworks, oh my god … greater then anyone has ever seen … explodes with the heat of a thousand rays, hotter than the sun, and it suddenly consumes my entire body, my entire being … oh my god … and then … I feel the heart beat of your now hot explorer shake with every burst of fire … oh baby, hurry home. My soul, my being, trembles just thinking of you …*"

There was a short pause, and then I let out a long sigh.

Princess and Pretty were both lying on their backs, sweating and breathing slightly fast. Not one of them said a word; they just laid there silently with their eyes closed.

Knock, knock. Suddenly, I heard a loud voice say, "Time to get up, Precious, it's eight o' clock."

2. Princess
(A P in a New Pod)

Princess, the eldest of three sisters, had just gotten married in August to a man named King Malech. They made a wonderful couple. Both were into the banking business. King was a vice president, and Princess had received her second promotion, to a senior executive financial officer. The good thing about their jobs; they were in different banks altogether.

Now Princess was a twenty-six-year-old virgin when she got married, and amazingly, King wasn't very experienced either. He was twenty-six. The thing they both had in common was that they both felt royal and loved to look and act that way as well. It was truly something that came natural for them both; it wasn't a put-on. King drove a silver gray Mercedes and Princess a black Lexus coupe, 2009. They would drive only the latest.

Princess went to work every day in her designer suits—Tahari, Michael Kors, Tracey Reece, etc.—and name brand shoes like Jimmy Choo. Her hair and nails were always done as if she was a movie star. King was the same, wearing imported Oscar de la Renta and Armani suits with Italian and European imported name-brand shoes. They both looked like they came from money or something. Or maybe their parents were the king and queen of an entire country. You would never see them in the same clothes that they wore to work anywhere other than to work or business. When they went out, they looked like they were stepping on the red carpet. Even their play clothes looked royal. The average person would wear their play clothes to work sometimes.

Believe it or not, for two people to be so royal, they were two humble individuals. They weren't the type to look down on you or act as if they were better than you. They were real people. They made jokes and had fun; however, all these things were done very classy. Just being in their presence made you feel like you were in the *Coming to America* movie or something.

When King and Princess got married, they were very prepared. They rented a small, one-family house, furnished it, and had it waiting for after the wedding. They were smart and cautious; they rented first, but they had the option to buy it if everything worked out well, I guess, with them and the house. They knew deep down inside that everything would definitely work. However, they were smart enough to play it safe without really saying it to one another. These two had been together for four years. They met while Princess was doing her degree in a local college and King was working part-time at the college for extra money for his online PhD course. It was love at first sight for the both of them; they were a perfect match for each other.

Now Princess always had her sisters to talk with. She had one very good girlfriend that she grew up with, Sibble; however, she would talk intimate stuff only with her sisters, and Princess would never show that side of herself to anyone other than her sisters. The three sisters didn't really let other women into their world. It was a trust thing. They really only trusted each other. Princess, being the eldest, had made friends with Sibble when they were small. Oftentimes, Sibble appeared a bit jealous. She didn't really understand them, possibly because she didn't have any sisters. She had all brothers, four of them. Sibble had gotten married the year before, and she was, therefore, Princess's matron of honor. Pretty and Precious were her bridesmaids. She had her cousin's twins as her flower girl and ring bearer and all the other trimmings you could think of.

The night before the wedding, Princess and her wedding party were up talking all night with last-minute personal preparations. Princess was so nervous, contemplating more about the honeymoon than the actual wedding. The anticipation of making love had overwhelmed her. Every time one of her sisters or Sibble mentioned the honeymoon, Princess's stomach would jump like horses over a large fence, and she would stop in her tracks and bend over. Everyone would laugh so hard, but she didn't think it was so funny.

Her mother, Penene, had come into the room to make sure everything was going well, and she heard them laughing. When Penene saw Princess bent over, she asked if she was all right, and the girls laughed even harder. Princess was looking very ill. Her mother went over to her and asked her to come with her and not to listen to her sisters. "They're crazy," her mother said to her, "especially Pretty."

Penene was holding Princess around the waist and led her to the den. Penene spoke to Princess, explaining that she would be all right and she could trust that. Penene also told her daughter that she knew what was wrong with her. A bit embarrassed, Princess just looked up at her mother. Penene then asked Princess if she didn't think that she felt the same way the night before her own wedding. She too had been a virgin. Penene explained how she was even greener then her girls, and she didn't have a sister like Precious with all those luscious and passionate stories. Princess looked up at her mother in shock. Penene said, "Yes, I know, I've heard some of her stories. That girl is good; she should become a professional writer or something." Penene then burst out laughing. Princess laughed along with her. Princess said if Precious knew her mom had heard some of her stories she would die. Penene then said to Princess that she should never mention it, that it would be their secret.

Penene went over and sat next to Princess. She then recounted the night before her wedding, when she couldn't stop shaking. Every time she thought about her honeymoon, she cried and even wanted to call off the wedding. She was terrified. The worst thing about the entire time was that while she and her sisters were close, they did not speak about such things; it was taboo. She was out there all by herself, to wonder and be terrified.

Princess just listened very attentively and sympathetically. Finally that night came, even though she tried to delay it for a week or a month, and then, it was nothing.

Princess looked up very puzzled at her mom. What did she mean by nothing? Penene was just staring with a blank look on her face and she said again, "Nothing." She explained that she didn't feel a thing, plus she didn't even remember a thing about that night. Penene expressed that she felt she might have been in a coma or something, but there was nothing. Truthfully, she explained that she didn't think she really felt anything until she was much older, maybe even after she had had Princess. Princess then questioned her mom: "You must have felt something?" Penene was very serious when she answered Princess, explaining that there was so much anticipation and then there was nothing. Penene explained that she did not want her to get the wrong idea; she had had a very good time exploring over the years. Princess shut her eyes and asked her mother not to give her too many details; she was still her mother. Penene smiled.

Penene told her baby girl not to worry about it; it would be all right. Just remember how it was when she were about to take an exam in school, she would study and study because she thought the test would be so hard, and didn't think she would pass, and then what happened? She would come home screaming, "Mom, dad, the test was so easy" and how she knew she had passed. She told her that night would be the same way, and she would pass with flying colors. King loves her and she loves him. That means everything will fall into place, it will be fine. Princess slowly laid her head on her mother's lap, and her mother started rubbing her back. Penene then said to Princess, "I hope you're not expecting all those things that your sister talks about, because she may be very disappointed." Both Penene and Princess started laughing. Princess was thinking how she would love to experience some of those things.

The morning of the wedding madness had begun; but everything went beautifully and the reception was truly a blessed event. Princess and King looked just like they were the Queen of England's children; they were dressed so royally and beautifully. Someone called the local media after spotting the wedding party getting out of the limousines; the locals thought they were famous people. Mr. & Mrs. King Malech's pictures showed up in the local newspapers; none of their family or friends was surprised.

When it was time to leave the reception, Princess quietly tried to stay until the end, but King kept telling her he was tired. Her sisters Pretty and Precious kept asking her "when are you leaving". Finally, the time came, and they were leaving for their new home, to change their clothes, grab their bags, and head for the airport. As they were leaving, the guests blew bubbles, and someone let loose seven white doves. It was so romantic and beautiful. The doves were a surprise from her sister Precious. As they got into the antique limo, Princess's sisters kissed her on the cheek, and Precious whispered in her ear, "Relax and let yourself enjoy love," and gave her a big hug.

When Mr. and Mrs. Malech entered their honeymoon suite, in Hawaii, it was breathtaking. The colors, the flowers, the view of the ocean, were indescribably beautiful. Princess ran out on the balcony and yelled for King to come quick; she wanted him to see how beautiful everything looked from the balcony. King went out on the balcony and grabbed Princess around the waist, gently yet firmly; Princess suddenly found herself very weak in her knees and leaned over on the balcony. King was very concerned and asked if she was all right. Princess answered that she was fine, just a bit tired from that long flight. King agreed with her that the flight was pretty long. Princess went to walk inside, and King grabbed her again and started kissing her very passionately. Princess felt as if she wanted to faint, but she held on to him very tight. Suddenly, she pushed him away and said, "Take it easy, we'll have a lifetime." King answered that he wanted to start enjoying his lifetime now and asked if she was as eager to start also. Princess looked at King and said she would go take a shower; she asked if he was hungry. King questioned Princess about all the food they had eaten on the plane. He then expressed that he was hungry, but not for food.

Princess opened her suitcase, took something out, and went into the bathroom. King looked around, and then he too took some things out of his suitcase and went into the other bathroom. King came out smelling fresh with a towel wrapped around his waist; as he went over to the bed, he noticed beautiful rose petals all over the king-size bed. It was so romantic. King walked over and opened the balcony doors wide and the smell of the ocean was so heavenly, he just went out and sat down on a chair, awaiting his bride.

King had only had one close encounter with a woman, but he didn't have a condom so he never went all the way. However, he is a man and he was instinctively very brave and willing to get started.

Now Princess was in the bathroom, looking in the mirror, making sure everything on her was just right, but in reality, she was stalling. She was terrified and did not want to come out of the bathroom. She sat down and started thinking about the story her mother had told her, and a smile came over her face. Then she asked herself, did she want her night to just be OK, or did she really want what her sister dreams about? She did not really know. Princess jumped up, looked into the mirror, and thought to herself that she had to go through with it: she looked beautiful, she was in a beautiful place, and she had to get through it. Princess took a deep breath and then bravely opened the door.

Princess walked out of the bathroom; she was wearing a sheer satiny, royal purple short robe with nothing underneath, looking and smelling awesome. King heard her come out and when he turned his head to see her; he stood up almost in shock. He had never seen his bride in this way, and she looked so beautiful and ready for his picking. They looked at each other, and Princess started trembling uncontrollably. She tried to hide it from King, but he noticed. He gave her a serious look of calm and walked over to her, grabbed her hands gently, and said to her, "Princess baby, relax, it will be fine, we do have a lifetime together, please relax." Princess then assured him that she was fine, just a little nervous of the unknown, and she smiled.

King held his bride's hand and led her on the balcony; he wanted to see her in all the beauty surrounding her. Princess followed like a little girl, still shaking. She stood up, and King put his arms around her waist and started to kiss her neck. Princess wanted to melt straight down to the sea; instead she just closed her eyes. King had kissed her like this so many times before, but she had never felt the way she felt at that moment. She knew this time it was very different; she knew he would get to go all the way with her, and that feeling alone had her terrified.

King turned her around and started kissing her hard, yet gently, and rubbing her from head to waist. He stopped for a moment and just looked at her, then he pulled the string on her robe, and there she was in her natural, beautiful state. King suddenly and slowly lifted his bride and carried her to the beautiful bed awaiting them. He laid her down gently and just stared at her beauty. Princess laid down with her eyes closed; she would not look at him, and she trembled even more. King's voice was all that Princess heard. He laid on top of her and whispered, "Relax, baby." King then told her that he loved her and he would not hurt her in any way, and if she wanted him to stop she should just say it, and he would. Princess nodded submissively.

At that instant Princess became brave, but she still wouldn't open her eyes. King slowly and sensuously started kissing her on her face and then slowly down to her breasts, caressing her nipples with his tongue slowly. He kept moving down and down, to her belly button. Princess was on fire inside, with her eyes shut ever so tightly. King kept reassuring his bride that it was going to be all right and she should relax.

He gently caressed her body, head to toe, kissing her lips, her breasts, her thighs all the way down to her toes; he caressed her toes in a manner that she had never imagined; Princess felt like she was about to explode. Each time King did something different to her body, she thought, *Oh Lord,* the feeling was so great, but each time it got even greater. Princess felt herself slowly drifting off, and all she heard was her sister Precious's soft voice describing everything that King was doing to her body. Princess then allowed him to take over, as any obedient queen would do. She remembered the last thing her sister had told her, "Relax and let yourself be loved," so Princess lay helplessly. The shaking had stopped, and a feeling of ecstasy came over her as she began to sigh ever so sweetly, and suddenly she began to move her shoulders and then her hips and then she could not stop, nor did she want to. Princess had then become the queen, and she rolled her King over. King was shocked; he looked a little nervous himself at first, but Princess started to do the same things to him that he had done to her, and boy was King shocked. He laid and felt his queen slowly drive him insane, until he couldn't take it anymore. King then whispered softly in Princess's ear, "Are you ready?" and she answered, "Yes baby, I'm ready."

King slowly turned his queen over and gently went on top; as he softly opened her legs with his leg, he kissed her nipples slightly, then her neck, and as his sweet Queen Princess laid with her eyes closed, King finally entered her kingdom. He pushed the gate gently and went inside; his queen let out a yell as if someone had blown a welcoming trumpet, and then King slowly, yet softly, tiptoed around inside until his queen was comfortable seeing and feeling him. When they were both comfortable she began to skip with him; King began to run, running from side to side, wall to wall, and suddenly he slowed down again. King slowed down but the queen was still running and panting as if he were chasing her, and that is exactly what the King did; he chased his bride up and down, round and round, until suddenly he caught her and she caught him. Princess's legs were now shaking uncontrollably, and suddenly both King and Princess felt like they were bursting like two atomic bombs, and they both then yelled in ecstasy. A rainbow of colors flashed before Princess's eyes; she had never felt the way she felt at that moment, and her legs would not stop shaking. King was sighing and breathing so hard you would have thought they were really fighting. King then in a soft voice whispered to her, "I've waited so long for you; I didn't realize what I was missing." Princess, however, never said a word. She seemed to be somewhere else, or fast asleep.

Ironically, Princess had drifted off to a place where her sister had taken her several times before in one of her stories. She had now graduated, she finally understood, and the feeling was a thousand times more intense then the stories. She was truly in a land of ecstasy, and she didn't want to leave there at all. She sighed in her sleep.

King stared at his bride in utter disbelief. He had always thought of how it would really be his first time, but he had never imagined it would be to this magnitude. He thought about all the lustful things that a man could or would think of; however, that night he felt as though he had made love, love to the woman that he loved so much. King laid there with a stream of water running down the side of his eye as he looked at his bride.

3. Patrick and Penene
(Two P's That Made the Pod)

The families had gathered during the week of Princess and King's wedding. Penene had made plans with her two sisters (Michelle, a.k.a. Shelly, and Innis, a.k.a. Indy) for a weekend getaway to a health resort in the Poconos. The girls' father Patrick and his two brothers (Cadillac and Shawn) had planned their weekend at the casinos in Atlantic City. The two families made it their business to do something with their siblings every summer; this year it was a bit late because of Princess's wedding.

Now Penene, a.k.a. Pinky, was the youngest of her three sisters, and she was always very excited to be around them, but she did not like them using her nickname. Her sisters were very worldly and she was the baby, always under the protection of her big sisters. Ironically, she had no brothers and her husband had no sisters, and they loved to be around one another. In addition, Penene's second-oldest sister, Indy, was married to her husband's second-oldest brother, Shawn. Patrick was the baby of his brothers as well. When they all got together, they truly had a ball. The oldest two of both Patrick's and Penene's siblings were widowed and everyone was trying to hook those two up for years, but that's another story.

They all left for their weekend trip a few days after the wedding. While the three sisters were sitting in the hot tub in the Poconos, sipping glasses of wine, Indy was wondering how the married couple were doing on their honeymoon. Penene was sure they were fine, since no one loved each other more then those two. Shelly thought it was so sweet, remembering when her baby was alive. *Boy, were they in love,* she thought. Shelly had a real distant, sensual look on her face while she was reminiscing. Penene laughed at her sister and explained that she realized where her daughter the dreamer gets all that intimate stuff from; it was from her. Indy asked Shelly, if she didn't think that she was too old to be having those thoughts, especially since her husband was dead. Shelly yelled out that her husband was dead but she wasn't. Shelly wanted to know what was wrong with her sisters and why were they so cold; did their husbands light fires for them?, because hers sure did and boy did she miss him. Shelly explained to her sisters that she did not think she would ever find someone like her baby Charles. Penene and Indy giggled like schoolgirls, and they both then said at the same time that they knew someone for her. Shelly shook her head and said, "Yeah, yeah! I know, Cadillac."

Shelly looked at the both of them for a moment while sipping her wine, and slowly expressed that she did not understand why they wanted her to join that family with them, since they were girls that did not seem to be too sexually alive. Penene and Indy looked very puzzled at one another and then they looked at Shelly. Indy told her sister that she was a sick woman, and that she knew that she herself was sexually alive; maybe it was Shelly or Penene that was dead sexually but it was definitely not her. Penene laughed, and then she asked them why they were putting her in their conversation; she was fine the way she was, and she thought that she too was alive. Penene asked out loud, "Aren't I?" Both Shelly and Indy laughed so hard that they were choking. Shelly then asked Penene if she was still a square in the bedroom. Shelly then told Penene she'd better start taking lessons from some of her daughters' stories; she'd be surprised how her sex life would improve. Penene had a look on her face of anger and curiosity but never said a word. Indy then suggested that they get out of the hot tub before they started to shrivel up like prunes. The sisters agreed and then grabbed their towels and headed for their room.

Later that evening the sisters got dressed and went out for dinner; they were as jolly as ever, laughing like three schoolgirls. All three were in their mid- to late forties, but all three looked very good, and that night they were dressed very strikingly and sexy, none of them looking their age. As they sat at the dining table sipping their wine, Penene seemed to be far away in thought. Shelly asked her baby sister what was wrong; she wanted to know what was on her mind. Penene replied that she was just thinking about her and why she wouldn't go out with Patrick's brother Cadillac, especially since he was looking for a good wife like her. He was financially stable, and he was in good health, Penene explained to her and then gave her a sweet girly smile. Indy chimed in, reiterating that he was a good guy, and she was already fond of his family. Shelly thought to herself, these two never give up. She then looked at Penene and said, "Don't give me that I'm thinking of you. I know you Pinky, something is bothering you, come on spill it." Pinky smiled and said that she knew they would laugh at her or think she was crazy if she told them and pleaded with them not to call her Pinky. Indy explained that she shouldn't think that way, if she has a problem, who best to talk to but her sisters, and then she said, "What is the problem?" Penene gave a big sigh, and looked up at her sisters somewhat embarrassed. Then she blurted out, "What is the difference between making love and having sex?" Indy expressed a sigh of relief, and asked Pinky if that was it; she really thought that she had a real problem. Penene then said, "Stop calling me Pinky, I'm not a little girl any more, Innis." "Please do not call me Innis, I prefer Indy, if you don't mind," replied Indy. Shelly then raised her voice a bit, telling the two of them to stop it, because they were sounding like children.

Shelly then turned to Penene, and said, "Listen, honey, there is a big difference between making love and having sex. Having sex is when someone jumps on you, do their business and it's slam bam thank you ma'am the same old way, it never changes. Making love is when you can reach your peak and he hasn't even entered your world. Oh sweetie, if you ever made love, you would know the difference, believe me." Indy was just listening, and inside she was thinking to herself, had she ever made love? Shelly looked over at Indy and asked, "What about you, have you ever made love?" Indy smiled and said, "I think so, and especially if I'm drinking or something, I think I have exploded a few times, but the rest of the time I think I fake it." Shelly responded, "Oh my Lord, and you people want me to get into this family, maybe I should just help you guys out. I know when I get finished with Cadillac, he would spread the word to his brothers and all your lives would be exciting." "Oh stop it, Shelly, we're happy with our husbands," sighed Indy. "I'm not saying you're not happy, but I know you would be damn satisfied if they were doing something right, but if you don't know, then you would never know if it's right or not," said Shelly.

"What are you suggesting, Shelly, we should go out and try it with someone else?" said Penene. "No way, that's not what I'm saying, I'm saying read a little more, not history books, but love stories, talk to your husband, try something different, experiment. What is wrong with you prudes? Don't you ever wonder what certain things would be like, or feel like? Get with it! Charles and I were married for twenty something years and we experimented and explored each other. We had an exciting love life; we didn't have to do the same thing all the time and that's what made it even more exciting. I can tell you, I have exploded a thousand different ways, no, a million different ways. I have made love in so many ways and yes, I have had sex several times as well, but it was a mood or a choice. Listen, you each have a husband. That is the person you try all the things that you think are crazy. Other women go out and have affairs to fulfill their fantasies, men too. What they don't realize is that they could fulfill their fantasies right at home." Penene then asked, "Do you think Pat is having an affair?"

Shelly then said, "Oh my god, you are crazy and green, aren't you? Pat is probably just like you, a prude. Just because you both were virgins when you got married you got very comfortable with one another, and then you both stopped. You don't think you should or you're too old, etc. … but honey let me tell you, life begins when the children are grown. No more hiding to get a piece, thinking about if the children, when the children or the example you have to set for the children, it's all about you, you and your husband. You girls better enjoy it and explore it; it's yours and you want to keep it yours."

A voice then said, "Who gets the Caesar salad?" and their dinner began. Penene was eating her salad and still thinking about all the things her sister had said. They danced, drank some more wine, and turned in for the night, laughing and having a good time, for tomorrow they had to hit the road for home.

The sisters had a wonderful weekend, and for Penene this was the most informative weekend she had ever had, and her big sister was one person that she trusted very much. She had finally got some questions answered that she had been too embarrassed to ask. Now the question was, what would she do with the information? Penene thought about their conversation all the way home.

It was around two o'clock Sunday afternoon when Penene drove up to her house. Patrick's car wasn't in the driveway; neither was Pretty's or Precious's. She figured the girls were at the mall shopping and Pat wasn't back as yet from Atlantic City. Penene took her things out of the car and went inside straight to her room. For some strange reason she went right to a box she had in her dresser and took out a story that Precious had written a few years before. It was about a love affair between a husband and his wife. This story had always interested her and she read it from time to time. Penene started thinking, if Precious knew she had one of her stories she would die, but she opened it up anyway, as always, and started to read.

She started from her favorite part … *"Honey let's go on a date, as if we were just married," said Roy. "A date?" said Brenda. "Yeah, a date, like we were just married, hot and fresh, but the fun thing is that we won't be as stupid as we were when we first got married." Brenda just laughed and shook her head. "Bren, we have talked about a lot of things over the years but we never tried them, why?" "I don't know, fear you think." "Fear of what, not doing them right?", and they both started laughing. "I'm serious Bren, let's do it, go up to the Poconos or a honeymoon suite somewhere and live out our fantasies, I have some things I need to try and see how it feels." "Roy you're nuts, but I have some things I need to try as well." Putting his hands around her waist, he said, "Like what baby, what do you want to try on me?" Brenda started blushing and pushing him away. "OK Roy you convinced me, I'll go."*

Penene turned a few pages and laid back on her bed … *"Bren I want to hear you scream, not a pretend scream, a real scream." "You have to make me scream, Roy." "Tell me how, tell me where to touch you, tell me what feels good to you Bren, tell me." Then Roy started kissing her all over her neck and breast, Brenda held his head and stared it around her breast and down the middle of her stomach, and Roy just let his head be led, down it went close to the valley. In a soft whisper, Brenda said, "Yes Roy, yes Roy, oh yes Roy."*

At that moment, Penene heard a loud voice: "Neen, are you here?" She jumped up off the bed and folded the paper, threw it in the box, and started pulling clothes out of her bag. She then answered, "Yes hon, I'm in the bedroom." Patrick walked in with his bag, dropped it on the floor, and hugged and kissed his wife. Then they both said at the same time, "How was your weekend?" They both smiled. "Boy you can tell we been married for a while," Penene said. Patrick answered first: "It was good. We had fun, I even won some money." He pulled out a stack of money from his inside pocket. "Wow! How much did you win?" "Five thousand bucks, but I gave Cadillac and Shawn a thousand each," he replied. "That was nice of you," said Penene. "Yes, they would have done the same thing so I didn't mind," was his reply.

"What should we do with the rest," he said. "I don't know," and she paused a moment, looking into the mirror at the box. Penene hesitated and then said, "I know, *let's go on a date, as if we were just married.*" Surprised, Patrick said, "What did you say?" "You heard me Pat, *let's go on a date, as if we were just married,* young and fresh." Patrick then jokingly said, "Hey girl! What did you do over the weekend? Are you sure you went to a spa with your sisters?" Then he started walking toward his wife, laughing and grabbing her. Penene's voice changed a bit, and she said, "Pat, you're crazy. I'm serious, I've been thinking about spicing up our love life." Patrick looked at Penene in utter amazement, and realized that she was very serious. Penene then asked her husband, "Do you think we have sex or make love?" "Wow! You're really serious," said Patrick and he sat on the side of the bed. In that instant they heard a couple of loud voices saying, "Mom, Dad, where are you?" Patrick looked over at Penene and said, "We'll finish this conversation later. At that moment Penene looked as if she had lost a little of her courage, and she looked away and said doubtfully, "Yes, later Pat, later."

Later that night after Patrick had taken his shower, Penene was in the bed already, checking some mail. When he got in the bed, he put his arms around his wife while lying on his stomach and said, "Now what was all that talk earlier about a date." Panene chicken out and said, "Nothing, forget it, it was nothing." Patrick grabbed her closer to him and said, "No I don't want to forget it, *Pinky I want to hear you scream, not a pretend scream, a real scream.*" Panene pushed his arm off of her and sat up, saying, "Why did you say that?" Pat started laughing. "I'm not laughing, Patrick, why did you say that?" insisted Penene. Patrick sat up and looked at his wife: "Penene, I've read Precious's writing also. Boy, that girl is good, don't you think? And yes, I read the one that is in your box also." Penene replied a bit angrily, "Patrick, you went into my things?" and he explained that he had found that one by accident one day.

Patrick then said, "The bottom line, Panene, is I wanted to

say something to you long ago, but I didn't know how." Panene turned and looked at Patrick, and he said to her, "As for your question earlier, do I think we have sex or make love, I think we have sex, but I think I'm ready now to make love to my wife. What do you think?" Penene looked at her husband while taking her arm out of her gown and said, "Make me scream, Patrick, make me scream," Patrick reached over, turned off the light, and put his head in Panene's hands, kissing her breast gently.

4. An Afternoon of Intimacy
(A P in a Pod)

It was a regular day. Precious was at work, and her class had gone on a trip. She stayed behind to enter the children's grades before parent-teacher's night the next week. While she was sitting at her desk, she happened to look up and Mike Gordon, a third grade teacher, was looking through the door smiling. Precious motioned for him to come in. Now Mike was always trying to talk to her, asking her out for dinner etc. For some reason Precious was not interested in Mike romantically; however, she would always talk with him. Mike entered her room smiling and saying, "Hey girl, are you almost finished? You look very busy, do you need some help?" Precious smiled back and replied, "No Mike, I'm fine, are you finished?" His reply was, "When are you going to go out with me, Ms. P, when?" "Oh Mike, aren't you tired of asking yet?" she replied. He rattled out quickly, "No, not yet, I have a few more years left to try," and he laughed softly. "Wow! That's a long time, are you sure you won't find someone else during that long wait?" said Precious. "I only have eyes for you, Ms. P, you know that," he replied. "Mike, go finish your work and let me finish mine, before my class returns." "OK, Ms. P, I'm leaving, but remember I'm still waiting for you." She just waved her hand, as he was leaving, saying, "Yes, I hear you Mike, I hear you."

Precious looked at the time and realized she had a few hours before the children returned, so she decided to go outside for a break. It was a nice fall day, not too cold, not too hot. All you needed was a light sweater; the weather was just right. She went and sat down on a bench in a nearby park that overlooked the schoolyard. There you could see the children and the people that walked by; she enjoyed sitting there. Precious sat down with her pad and pencil and just looked around for a minute. She saw a couple walking into the park holding hands and laughing, looking into each other's eyes as they walked. She thought that was so romantic. For an instant Precious thought, *soon that will be my husband/lover and I,* and she closed her eyes for a moment. She opened her eyes and looked up at the trees, lifted her pencil, and began to write.

Joy and her new husband Michael Peace had arrived at their all-inclusive exclusive honeymoon suite in St. Maarten, West Indies. The bellboy welcomed them, then grabbed their bags, saying, "Messier, your bungalow messier, is right to your left in that area, number 250," and he pointed to a very secluded-looking area right on the beach. You couldn't really see the bungalow; all you could see were beautiful flowers and small tropical trees. As they got to the bungalow you could see that it had a small grassy picnic area right to the side. It was so unique, the way it sat, sort of, down on the beach. No one could see you unless they came right up to the front door, but you could see anyone else before they saw you. It was beautiful. The bellman took the bags in, MP gave him a tip, and Joy ran straight to the water.

"Wait for me Joy, I'm coming," MP called, and he ran and caught his bride. Shoes came off, pants, blouse, and they were waddling around in the water, kissing and grabbing each other. MP went under the water and grabbed Joy from behind and she quickly turned around and wrapped her legs around his waist. At that instant Joy felt a very stiff sharpness, and suddenly her legs locked and she began to tremble. MP then said, "Madam Peace, are you all right? You have

locked me in." "Yes messier, I know, I want to keep you all to myself, in this position." "I have a better position for you; I think you will like it very much," he replied. At that moment Joy unlocked her legs and swam away, with MP right behind her. Joy got out of the water and ran toward the house, but he caught up with her; they wound up on the grass in between some beautiful colorful flowers, rolling around. The grass felt so warm and nice and MP just rolled on top of his bride. Joy just laid there with her eyes close feeling the warm sunrays on her face, in total submission.

He pulled the straps of her wet bra down and slowly started to caress his prize. This was the newlyweds' third encounter since the wedding; something had happened to their flight so they went to a local hotel until they could get out. Joy was a twenty-two-year-old virgin and Michael was a twenty-three-year-old virgin. Both were very much involved in their religious beliefs, and that was how they had met, two years ago.

MP started caressing Joy's body like the water does the sand; he'd go up a little and down all the way, Each time he went down, a piece of Joy went with him. As he caressed his wife, suddenly he entered another realm, one called paradise. He had gotten to what he had thought was paradise before, but this time, he realized that he had never really been there. Each time the ocean roared up on the sandbed, so did he, taking Joy with him, firmly but gently. He could hear the fish splashing in the ocean at the same time it roared. With each touch of her warm hands on his body, he roared even stronger. When he realized it, Joy was roaring with him, up the sand bed, and slowly, gently back down again.

Now, Joy had entered her own world where she heard birds singing love songs and dancing around the flowers and trees. Joy had entered nature's bedroom. As her warm body lay on the grass she felt the warmth of the earth, holding her up, keeping her from falling. She felt Michael's gentle lips on her every leaf and flower, and suddenly a firmness lifting her up toward the hot sun. Joy felt the rays of the heat, yet she did not burn; that heat entered her very soul, while at *the same time she could feel heaven sensing the heat and sending an ocean breeze to cool her off.*

After they both had enjoyed their individual journeys, they were destined to meet. Somewhere between the heavens and the sea, or the earth and the sun, these two souls dangled. Finally, they merged like the sun meeting the end of the ocean, after a hot summer's day. Encountering each other with the impact of a meteor crashing to earth, with the earth's floor holding them up with all of nature's force. Suddenly, the sound of the ocean roared even louder and the sun burned even hotter, the birds sang louder, and the colors of the flowers were illuminated with blinding beauty. At that very moment Michael and Joy had entered paradise together as one. The ecstasy was so overwhelming that Michael was trembling uncontrollably, while Joy started crying out to the heavens and the ocean, with an ever-so-grateful, lovingly thankful song.

The two lay side by side, touching, Michael looked at his bride, and she looked right back at him. Their lips then met with utter contentment and sincere gratitude, and their eyes closed. Joy's tears dried and Michael's trembling stopped, as they drifted off to sleep in the warm Caribbean breeze.

Precious held her pencil tight as she closed her eyes for a moment. "Ms. P, are you all right?" It was Michael. Precious looked somewhat embarrassed and started to pack her bag, saying, "I'm fine." "Are you sure?" asked Michael, "I saw you sitting here for a while. I thought you were writing; then I saw your eyes open and close like you were feeling ill, are you sure you're all right?" "I'm sure; I was just thinking and writing," she replied. "Ohhh, one of those stories I heard about, no doubt." Precious was somewhat annoyed and didn't answer him; she just started walking back toward the school. Michael then asked, "What were you writing? As Precious approached the entrance of the school gate she saw the bus pull up with her class. She looked at her watch and said, "Right on time." Ignoring Michael, she pushed past and went to greet her class.

5. A Secret Love Affair
(A P from a Pod)

The newlyweds decided to have their family over for an appreciation dinner and housewarming party. They were going to have two dinners, one for family and one for friends; their house wasn't large enough for both at the same time. Nothing too elaborate, but everything appeared elaborate that Princess and King did; they were just that way. Tonight they were expecting Princess's mom and dad, Panene & Patrick; her two sisters, Pretty and Precious; both of their aunts and both of their uncles; Shelly, Indy, Cadillac, and Shawn. Shelly's only son, Shelton, could not make it; he was in the Marines and was stationed overseas. They were also expecting Cadillac's only daughter, Morgan, and her Paris-born husband Jean Pierre, with their five-year-old twins Michael and Michelle; Indy and Shawn's two sons—J. J., nineteen, and E. Z., twenty—and Ma Sill and Pop Ray, Patrick's aunt and uncle, who lived in Florida, and who had raised him and his brothers.

The house was beautiful, and beautifully put together of course, with wood floors and chandeliers. The dining room had a spread of food as if it was thanksgiving. The den was set up for the children with games and cartoon DVDs. One thing about Princess and King: they never acted stuck-up; whatever they had, they didn't mind sharing. Importantly, they both loved their family very much.

The first to arrive that evening were Pretty and Precious. When Princess opened the door and saw her two sisters, all three screamed and hugged each other as if they hadn't seen each other for a year. Precious held Princess and then pushed her back to see if she looked different. Precious then said to her sister, "Yes, you look well loved my dear sister, well loved." Princess then said, "Don't start, Precious," with a huge smile on her face. Pretty laughed at her sister and started to look around the house. King then entered the room, looking very handsome as usual. He looked at his sister-in-law and said, "Hey sis" and hugged Pretty. Precious just looked at King with a grin on her face and he grinned back, until he said, "Come over here and hug me, girl, and stop it with those looks." Precious ran over and hugged her brother-in-law and then gave him a big kiss. Precious looked at the married couple and said, "I want to find love just like you two did, real love." King gently grabbed his new bride, put his hand around her waist, and said, "I pray you both find the love you're looking for because we sure did." The bell ran and King went to the door; it was Princess's cousin Morgan and her family. One by one the family started trickling in until they all were present.

Everyone was enjoying themselves nibbling and listening to music, looking at the wedding pictures, and talking about Princess and King's wedding day. Princess stopped the music and put in the DVD of the wedding. As they were watching the ceremony and laughing, Panene asked, "I wonder who will be next?" Indy looked at Shelly, and Patrick looked at Cadillac; everyone in the entire room started laughing. "They're still trying to hook us up, Shelly, what do you think?" said Cadillac. "Well, I think we should have a winter wedding, don't you, darling?" replied Shelly. Cadillac stood up to go get a drink, chuckling, "I think we should let the family decide, dear, they have everything else all mapped out." Shelly burst out laughing and went behind Cadillac to refill her drink also.

As the family continued to watch the wedding tape, Cadillac and Shelly found themselves fixing a drink together and then they walked out on the deck, where the moon was shining exceptionally bright. Cadillac looked over at Shelly as she was sipping her drink and staring out at the night. She had on a beautiful black sexy silk top, eloquently showing just enough cleavage, and a dark gray long pinstriped skirt, with some sexy black open-toe shoes. Shelly always dressed very well, and she looked very good in her clothes. Cadillac then asked, "What are you thinking about?" "Nothing," she replied. "Come on, Shelly, spill it, what are you thinking?" She then replied, "I'm just thinking how the family has been trying to hook us up for years now. Why didn't we ever hook up?" Cadillac, somewhat surprised, started staring into the night and smiling. "Your turn to speak up, spill it," said Shelly. "Why didn't we? We certainly had several opportunities." Cadillac just kept smiling, and Shelly tapped his arm gently and said, "Why are you smiling so much?" Cadillac turned and looked very romantically into Shelly eyes and said, "If you keep touching me, Shelly, I think we'll get married tonight." Shelly jumped back. "What did you say?" "You heard me, Shelly," Cadillac replied, and he walked away a bit. "Hey, don't walk away you chicken, what are you talking about?" said Shelly. Cadillac turned to Shelly and said, "Do you really want to know?" "Yes I do," she replied.

"Shelly, you are the sexiest, most sensual, caring woman I've seen in a long time, probably the only one since my Sandra. When I look at you my stomach starts to flutter; I feel like a schoolboy. Shelly looked at Cadillac and started blushing, and said, "What stopped you from telling me how you felt all these years?" Cadillac replied, "I wasn't sure how you felt and I didn't want to make a fool of myself." Shelly started to laugh; Cadillac then grabbed her hand and started moving closer toward her, when suddenly Michael ran out calling, "Grandpa, Grandpa, come here." Cadillac's eyes were shining as he looked into Shelly's and he let go of her hand. He turned and started speaking with his grandson Michael. Shelly just walked inside and joined the others; all the time her stomach was fluttering like butterflies were inside of it.

Indy looked over at Shelly and said, "Are you all right, sis?" "Actually, I'm feeling a bit tired, I think I'll hit the road," Shelly replied. Princess heard and said, "You can spend the night, you don't have to go home, auntie." "No dear, you guys are newlyweds; I won't do that, not now anyway," Shelley said. Shelly started getting her coat and kissing everyone good night. Cadillac walked into the room and casually kissed Shelly on the cheek and said good night. The two gave each other the same strange look, as though they were silently communicating with each other. Shelly secretly melted inside and couldn't wait to get home. When Jean Pierre heard Shelly saying good night, he told Morgan, "Maybe we better hit the road also; it is getting late and we have the children." They too started packing up to leave, when Cadillac said, "I better hit the road too." "Where are you going big brother, you don't have anyone waiting at home for you? Why not stay awhile," said Patrick. "How do you know who I have waiting?" Indy then said, "We can arrange to have someone waiting for you, and blinked her eye. Cadillac laughed and said, "No thank you, I'll make my own arrangements. Thanks family, love you, good night," and he went out the door.

Cadillac could not wait to leave; all he had on his mind was Shelly, who had left about thirty to forty-five minutes before him. He drove straight to Shelly's house and sat in the car for about twenty minutes thinking if he should or shouldn't go to the door. Finally, he worked up the nerve and got out of the car, went straight to the door and rang the bell. Shelly was expecting him, and casually went to the door, asking, "Who is it? It's me, Cadillac." She slowly opened the door and looked at him with a smile. "What took you so long?" Shelly was feeling very bold, as usual.

Shelly had his favorite drink ready on the table; a towel and robe were also waiting for him. Cadillac was shocked at Shelly's boldness, shocked and somewhat flattered. He grabbed her close to him and said, "You are pretty bold, Ms. Shelly, aren't you?" "Am I?" said Shelly. Cadillac grabbed her closer to him and started to kiss her like she never had been kissed before. His tongue felt so hot, hotter than anything she had ever felt before. Cadillac slowly started rubbing her back gently up and down. His hands were just as hot as his tongue and lips, unusually hot, like he had a fever or something; she could feel the heat through her clothes. Shelly began to sweat as if she was running in a race, her heart pounded, as she began to tremble. Suddenly, she felt like a virgin, somewhat afraid of what was going to happen next. The boldness she answered the door with, suddenly disappeared. She had turned into a shy little girl, not knowing what to do next, or where this man would touch her next. All she knew is that she wanted him to touch her. Cadillac was now in full control.

Cadillac let her go, kissing her softly on the lips; he then picked up his drink and towel and headed for the bathroom. Shelly was stunned and didn't know what to do next. She have known him over twenty something years, but this was a side of Cadillac she had no idea existed. Their families had been trying to hook them up for the past seven or eight years, Shelly thought to herself did I miss out all these years? She was daydreaming when Cadillac gently put his hand on hers and led her to the bedroom. Shelly had lost all her nerve, she didn't know what to do, so she decided to be led, and she eagerly followed this man that she knew for years and somehow trusted. Shelly stopped for a moment and said to him, "I need to ask you something." Cadillac looked at her and it was if he could read her mind, and said, "Yes, I do have some with me." Shelly said, "Thank you," and Cadillac replied, "I'm fine with that, I fully understand."

Cadillac led her to the bed and laid her down gently, and then he slowly laid beside her. Shelly's heart was pounding; she was afraid to turn and look at him. He gently put his hot hands on her body, exploring every inch of this beautiful newfound candy. For a moment Shelly had become a cherry-flavored lollipop, and that was Cadillac's favorite kind. He began to lick his lollipop up and down, everywhere, slowly to savor the flavor, but with each lick of his hot tongue, his pop began to melt quickly.

Tasting her cherry pop, Cadillac could not wait to visit Shelly's sweet shop. He was very eager to visit and he knew exactly what he wanted; that was everything she had to offer. Cadillac slowly approached the door with confidence, and for the first time in Shelly's life, she was afraid to open the door. The look that she saw in Cadillac's eyes was so intense it caused her to hesitate. Shelly could tell that Cadillac was a connoisseur and he sensed her fear, so he gently touched her and gave her a look that told her that everything would be all right. Shelly relaxed somewhat and then slowly opened the door and let Cadillac inside.

She had never had anyone enjoy her sweet shop as much as Cadillac. While he was enjoying himself, she enjoyed herself just as much with him. Only two people had visited her shop before, and one was her late husband William, but she could tell Cadillac was an experienced shopper. He didn't come in like a hungry man tossing things everywhere; he respectfully took his time not to miss a single thing. He handled everything gently and with sincere care. I mean everything; so much so, that Shelly was exhausted. As he was leaving, after an exhausting shopping spree, Cadillac was every shop owner's dream; he bought everything and paid in full, with cash. Shelly was so exhausted and shocked that when he left the shop she passed out cold.

Poor Cadillac was so nervous and exhausted himself, when he realized that Shelly was out cold, he ran and got some water and dabbed it on her face. Shelly laid with such a smile of contentment on her face; all Cadillac could do was hold her in his arms. As he held her close to his chest, he kissed her forehead and gently rubbed his hand over her cheek as if she were a baby. Cadillac looked up toward heaven and started crying; he could not believe how he felt at that moment. He had been so lonely lately and he now felt complete. This was the first time since Sandra that he had ever had the feeling that he had at that moment. As he thought about it, he realized he had never had this feeling even with Sandra; it was a first time for him. Tears started rolling down his face onto Shelly's face, and she opened her eyes. As she opened her eyes, tears rolled down her face as she looked up at him. They both just looked at each other for a second until they grabbed each other, hugged, cried, and started touching and kissing each other's faces. They could not believe what had just happened. Was it really real, did it just happen? They both finally drifted off to sleep in each other's arms, after crying, hugging, and kissing and thanking God.

When the morning came, the two took another brief trip to the shop; it was a refresher of their trip last night. They showered together and sat down at the table for breakfast. All they could do was smile; it was as if they had been together for years. Cadillac then said to Shelly, "So what do we tell the family? Shelly smiled, "I don't think we should say anything right now, they are so nosey, let them stew for a while."

Cadillac then said, "A while? You mean until we pick a date"? "A date for what?" replied Shelly. Cadillac looked at her with a warm smile. "Our wedding."

6. Did Pretty Meet Her Match?
(A P in the Pod)
Part One

It was the end of a long school day and there was no work the next day, school would be closed for a local holiday. Pretty was all packed to go work out at the gym. Working out had become her way of winding down after a long day at work. She also wanted desperately to stay in shape. She would always say how she wanted to stay in shape for her wedding day. Pretty did not want to be like some brides, trying to lose weight two months before the big day. She oftentimes wondered if she would ever get married; she knew her sisters would, but she wasn't too sure about herself. Pretty seemed to have a hard time when it came to dating, or just talking with men. Whenever a man tried to talk to her, it would go well for a while and then he was gone. Her family thought she scared them off, because she spoke so rough and acted so tough. However, they all knew she was really very sweet but misunderstood. Pretty would talk about the men when they didn't call her back; she would say they were just too soft. That is why she wanted a man that was a real man, strong, and able to handle her. If he couldn't handle her, he wasn't really a man, that was her explanation. Precious would always laugh at Pretty; she would tell her, when she really finds the right man she would probably melt and wouldn't know what to do.

As Pretty was packing her bag to leave work, a male co-worker passed by her classroom door and smiled at her. He had caught her off guard with his smile. She barely looked at him, and never really smiled back; she just wasn't the smiling type. As she grabbed her bag to leave, her friend Gwen Parker, a computer teacher, came by. She asked." Are you going straight to the gym, Ms. P?" "Yes I am. What do you have in mind for tonight?" Pretty asked. "Well my brother called and asked if we wanted to go on a blind dinner date tonight." "A blind dinner date in the middle of the week? Oh no, not me," said Pretty. Gwen explained that her brother had two friends that just moved to the area a few months ago, two SPMs. Pretty started laughing, "SPMs?" "Yes girl, Single Professional Men." "What profession, and why don't they have women, what's wrong with them?" asked Pretty. "I don't know but it beats the online dating, at least you can see who and what you are talking to. Do you want to go?" said Gwen. "I don't think so, I'm going to the gym, and I need to work out tonight." "You are always working out, take a break," said Gwen. "I hate blind dates, you know that, you need to be blind to go on a blind date, it always turns out to be disastrous," said Pretty. "Plus, tomorrow we have that 'Mix and Mingle' brunch at the center, did you forget? I told Precious I would go with her. She bugs me about it every time it comes around, and I promised her. I'm glad you mentioned it, I had forgotten all about it," said Gwen. The two then parted for the night.

The next day Pretty awoke to a cool sunny day and no work. She had gotten up early, and she and Precious were getting ready to go to the singles brunch. It was an every-other-month affair for singles, a way to meet and network. Pretty thought it was a waste of time and didn't really like going. However, Precious did, and she always managed to convince Pretty to tag along with her. Pretty was always talking, or thinking about, having sex with a real man. Precious thought she should find a husband fast so she would stick to their agreement. Pretty did not understand why men and women didn't experiment before marriage. She thought about all those men and women who were stuck with mates that did not satisfy them. She was always afraid of that happening to her. Precious, on the other hand, was always looking for love. She believed when a person finds love, she would not have to worry about sex, because everything would fall into place. As much as Pretty wanted to believe that, she was still afraid. Ironically, she was more afraid to have sex before marriage or even before falling in love with someone. The thought of a negative outcome frightened her more. Pretty would always hear her parents' voices in her head saying, "It's the only thing you have, it's precious and once you give it away you can't get it back. Don't let any old person get it, save it for someone really special, someone that is really willing to stick around and wait for it, no sex before marriage …" Then it was her pact with her sisters, "No sex before marriage, it's ours, that is all men want." Even though she always thought about experimenting, she never really found anyone that she really felt could handle her or anyone she really wanted. Pretty wanted a "MAN," a real man, strong in every way. So even though she didn't like going to these singles things, she went,, She felt you never really knew what could happen, plus she loved being around Precious, who always took Pretty on an sexual adventure or a intimate fantasy ride somewhere. Precious was always looking for love and Pretty knew she was looking for sex, maybe, or love or something. Pretty was never really sure what she truly wanted.

As the girls got ready to leave, their father Patrick was on his way out to go golfing. He looked at his two daughters and started laughing. Precious asked what was so funny. "You and your sister," he replied. "Pretty looks like someone is forcing her out and you look like you're going to pick up a prize," he continued. Precious started to laugh with her father as she looked around at Pretty. Precious then said, "You know Pretty is always looking for a fight." Pretty then looked at the two with a smile and said, "Dad, you know I'm just going with Precious while she finds her dream lover," and she started laughing aloud. Patrick replied that both girls were silly, and wished them good luck. Both girls yelled, "Enjoy your game, Dad" as he got into his car.

The girls arrived at the center about thirty minutes early. The men and women always met separately first. They would meet in separate rooms to pray before going to mix and mingle over brunch. Some of the women were serious about their prayers because they really wanted to find a mate, while others just come out to be nosey, or just to see who was available and network. Like Pretty, she did not think she would find anyone at these affairs. While Precious, on the other hand, kept her options open, she was always searching for her true love.

There were approximately fifteen women present, and they were chatting away when the girls arrived. As they walked in, Linda Cherry shouted, "Hey Precious, you ready to find your dream lover today?" Precious smiled and then started kissing and hugging the other women. Pretty was ready to say something to Linda when Precious looked at her and said, "Please behave yourself, would you?" Pretty smiled, "No problem, mommy, I'll behave." Pretty then spotted her co-worker Gwen; she went straight over to her and said, "Good morning, desperate woman, are you ready for your mate?" with a big smile on her face. Gwen just looked at Pretty and said, "Stop acting like you don't want to find someone too, I know better." Pretty replied, "Of course I want to find someone, but I don't think it will be here. These guys are religious and wimpy, and I want a man, a real man." "Real man?" said Gwen. "Why can't real men be religious or spiritual? Never mind, don't answer that, your mind is in the gutter anyway, Pretty." "No it isn't, I'm a realist and a twenty something-year-old virgin, and my body is screaming all the time," said Pretty. "The sad thing is your mouth screams just as loud as your body and you run potentials away," said Precious, laughing. Gwen and Pretty both looked around at Precious and started laughing.

Sister Marjorie then said, "Can I have everyone's attention

please? I'm so happy to see so many of you out this morning, especially you, Pretty." All the women started clapping and shouting, "Yes, we're so happy" and laughing. Pretty just bowed and smiled along with them. "On a serious note, ladies, we all know why we're here this morning. I would like to begin our session with a prayer this morning before we go to mix and mingle over brunch.

"Lord we humbly come before you this morning, giving you thanks and praise for our very being, for waking us up in good health and in our right mind this morning. Lord, we come before you to ask that you be with us, and as you created Eve for Adam, we pray that the Adam you create for us is here this morning. We pray that our Adam be one with you, that our Adam be as Abraham with Sarah, and as Isaac with Rebecca. We pray that we meet our soul mate this morning, each and every one of us. But most of all, dear Lord, we pray that all be done as you see fit, in your appointed time. Give us the patience and the faith to wait on you, and we will continue to give you the honor, the praise, and the glory forever and ever Halleluyah. Amen."

Then Sister Marjorie said, "Are you ready, ladies? It's eleven o'clock, let's go," and the women all headed for the lunchroom. When they arrived, they all looked stunned. There were so many men, at least twenty-five or more; this was a first. The women were pleasantly shocked; they had so many choices. Both the men and the women looked at each other with big bright smiles. At that moment the food was being rolled in on trays and lined up. Everything looked so delicious and colorful; fresh flowers were on every table and there was plenty of food. Everyone was dressed and just as fresh looking as the flowers and the fruit on the trays. The sun was shining through the windows so brightly and there was soft music playing in the background. The atmosphere was very appropriate for mixing and mingling.

Suddenly a voice said, "Good morning, ladies and gentlemen, and welcome to our sixth Mix and Mingle brunch. We would like to say a prayer over our meal before we get started, and then we will ask that you enjoy your meal, mix, mingle, and prayerfully you'll meet a lifelong friend. Please remember, don't get discouraged if you don't meet a mate today. Just remember to network, meet new friends, and do not be discouraged. This may be the route to which you find your mate. Remember, everything happens in God's appointed time. With that, I would like to ask our new brother Malcolm from New York City to give us a prayer." Malcolm looked up from almost in the back of the room. He was somewhat surprised; however, he gave a look as if to say, "No problem," and then lifted up his hands and began to pray.

"Father, we come before you this morning to give thanks for this food that was prepared for us, and to give thanks for the preparers. We ask that you be with each and every one of us, for the nourishment to our bodies and our minds. Father, we pray that you continue to watch over us and guide our spirit to the place it should be this morning. Amen"

The entire room was silent as Malcolm prayed. His voice echoed through the room; it sounded strong yet soothing, and all the women wanted to know who this person was. Everyone headed toward brunch and the mixing and mingling had officially begun. Of course most of the women had their eyes on Malcolm, and they were working their way across the room toward him. Now Malcolm was a handsome man, tall, about six feet three, handsome and thick but not big. His eyes looked like those of a firm dreamboat, serious yet gentle. His presence was manly and suave at the same time. He was dressed in a casual, but smart style. He had on jeans, a designer blazer and a cool-colored shirt with soft-bottomed shoes. Malcolm looked very classy and professional, but down to earth. At least ten of the fifteen women were really eyeing him. Precious was speaking to Lynn, a longtime friend of hers, and Pretty was teasing Gwen because she was drooling over Malcolm but she couldn't get close to him, because a sister named Stephanie had gotten to him first. Pretty thought the entire scene was amusing.

As they moved closer to the food trays, two handsome men

came over to both Gwen and Pretty, saying, "Good morning, ladies. I'm Cliff and I'm Martin." They stuck out their hands, Cliff to Pretty and Martin to Gwen. Pretty looked uninterested of course and Gwen was excited and open. She and Martin started to talk, and Cliff started talking to Pretty as she started selecting her food. The four got their food and sat at a table. At that moment Precious came over and sat down, and a nice little man with a warm smile came next to her and said, "May I join you? Precious looked up with a smile. "Sure, have a seat. I'm Precious." He smiled at her and said, "Yes you are," and everyone started laughing. "My name is Johnson," and he smiled. He looked like he was mesmerized by Precious, and she just smiled at everyone, so it was hard to tell if she was interested. Precious looked like she was somewhere else during the conversation anyway, probably daydreaming again. She had a way of physically being in your presence but mentally being in her own world.

As they were talking about their professions and other things, Gwen's eyes were still on Malcolm, when suddenly, someone came behind her and put their hands over her eyes, Pretty and Precious started to say something, but the person gave the shhh sign to them. "What are you doing here?" he said. It was her brother Eric. "I didn't know you were coming."

"I didn't know you were coming either," said Gwen. "I was here the last time," Eric said; suddenly he looked up and went chasing the sister named Linda. Cliff and Pretty got into a heavy conversation about politics, Gwen and Martin both got up and started to talk to other people, while Johnson was just talking and talking to Precious and she was somewhere else totally.

Precious was daydreaming again; there she *was walking into an empty ballroom, and there her lover was standing with his hands stretched out, just waiting for her to join him. Her heart was pounding as he reached out and clasped her two hands and they started to dance, everything in her body was ticking, beating like drums, from her head to her toes, her legs trembled so much she could barely stand to dance. Her inner thighs quivered and her knees dared to stand firm. However, this gift from God twirled and twirled her unto she fell safely into his arms; there the two spirits were joining like the sun pressing against the sky. As this wonderful vision of man gently put his lips to hers, a fire rose up with flames shooting straight to the heavens. At that moment Precious started to melt like ice cream on a hot summer day, dripping down on every side ... and as she oozed down on every side, this wonderful figure, this epitome of a man started to lick every drop as not to let a single drop go to waste ...*

"Hello! Hello! Precious." "Yes," answered Precious with a big smile on her face, her legs clinched tightly together under the table. "I didn't know if you heard me," said Johnson. "I'm sorry," she said, "would you excuse me for a moment?" "Sure," he replied. Precious got up and started walking toward the trays; she just had to get up and walk, or something. She hadn't heard a word that Johnson had said for the past ten or fifteen minutes. Pretty saw the look on her face and excused herself from Martin to join her sister. Gwen was still trying to make her way over to Malcolm. She spotted her brother talking with Malcolm and Gloria, so then she made her way over to them. Gwen introduced herself to Malcolm as Eric's sister, and he smiled with his flashing white teeth and said, "Yes, I know, I didn't have the opportunity to formerly meet you." Gwen was so wrapped up in shaking his hand that she never paid attention to what he was saying. Suddenly, Malcolm seemed a bit preoccupied with something and wasn't really paying much attention to the conversation. Gwen kept talking and talking, as her brother eased away to a table with Gloria, who was smiling from ear to ear with him. Malcolm apologized and excused himself from Gwen, saying, "I'm sure we'll speak again, please excuse me for a moment," and walked off.

On the other side of the room Precious and Pretty were talking about Precious daydreaming everywhere. Precious didn't care at all; she just smiled and smiled. Pretty was amazed how Precious could tune out everything and just daydream. Pretty told her she was ready to leave; it was a waste of her time being there. Precious smiled and told Pretty to relax, since it would be over soon. She then walked off and left Pretty standing alone. Pretty looked around and then walked toward a side window overlooking some beautiful old trees. She was admiring the scenery and thinking what a ridiculous waste of time and a wasted day this was; she would have had a better time golfing with her father.

In that instant, a soft, confident, and soothing voice said, "Good afternoon, lovely lady," but Pretty never turned around; she just continued to gaze out the window. Again, the voice said, "Good afternoon, lovely lady." Pretty then turned around and there was Malcolm standing, looking straight into her eyes. For the first time in Pretty's life she was speechless; she just stared, somewhat shocked. He held out his hand and said, "Hi, I'm Malcolm." Pretty just stood there frozen as he said it again: "Hi, I'm Malcolm." Finally, she said, "Hello, I'm Pretty." Malcolm said, "Yes, I see," looking her up and down. "May I ask what you find so fascinating out the window?" Pretty never answered; she turned and continued to stare nervously out the window. Malcolm's soothing, strong, manly voice seemed to have hypnotized her or something.

Precious then walked up to the two of them. "It's Malcolm, right?" Yes it is, how are you?" said Malcolm. "I'm Precious, this young lady's sister." Precious then gazed over at Pretty and Pretty had a strange look on her face, one that Precious had never seen before. "Are you all right, Pretty?" "Yes, I'm fine." Precious then said, "Do you want to sit down or something? You don't look so good." Malcolm then said, "I'll get you some water" and walked away swiftly. Precious looked at Pretty and held her arm. Pretty was trembling, and her hands were so clammy. Precious said to her, "Let's sit down, you really don't look so good. Are you sure you're all right?" They then sat down at the nearest table. Malcolm returned with a glass of water; he had a very concerned and serious look on his face as he handed the cup to Precious to give to her sister. Pretty looked up at him, and then quickly looked away. Precious sat looking puzzled for a moment; then she suddenly realized what was wrong with her sister. Precious looked at Pretty, looked at Malcolm, and then said, "I'll be right back." Pretty gave her sister such a look, a look saying "You'd better not leave me here with him alone," but Precious smiled, got up, and walked away toward Gwen and Eric. Malcolm looked at Pretty, and asked her, "Are you all right now, do you feel better?" For the first time, in a soft, very feminine voice, Pretty answered, "Yes, I'm fine, thank you."

Malcolm then said, "I must confess, Ms. Pretty, I've been trying to meet you for the past five months. I see, hear, and smell you almost every day at work. I've been trying to go on a blind date with you for the past three months; you are a very hard woman to get to know." Pretty looked shocked and somewhat amazed. "Yes," said Malcolm, "I work at the same school; I pass by your class and smile at you every day and every afternoon. I am one of Eric's friends from New York. My friend, Chauncey and I relocated here about six months ago, and we were the two men that wanted to go on a blind date with you and Gwen last night."

Pretty looked into his eyes and melted; she looked around the room in embarrassment, and she saw Gwen, Precious, Eric, and Chauncey talking and smiling. She could not believe what she was hearing or feeling. It all seemed like one of Precious's love stories. She had never felt the way she was feeling at that moment. Her stomach was turning nervousness, her hands were sweating, and her heart was beating so fast as if it was trying to catch someone. Every part of her body was trembling in a different direction. An unexplainable heat was traveling through her body. She didn't know what to do or say, so she just sat there frozen at the sound of his voice. Malcolm then touched Pretty's hand. She was shaking almost uncontrollably, and he said, "So when can we go out to dinner tonight?" Pretty pulled back her hand gently and just looked at him. "So what do you say? I know you're not seeing anyone, Ms. Pretty, no, Ms. Gorgeous, so what do you say, tonight?" Malcolm looked her straight in her eyes, pulled out a pen from his pocket, and wrote down his telephone number on a napkin. "I know this might be a bit subtle for you, but here is my number. Call me when you're ready. I will definitely be waiting for you, I mean your call." Malcolm stood up reached for her hand again, and this time he gently kissed the back of it, as if she were a queen. He then walked straight to the other side of the room and out the door. Pretty sat there, with every organ in her body shaking. For the first time in her life, she was speechless in a daze.

7. Did Pretty Meet Her Match?
(A P in a Pod)
Part Two

Mixing and mingling was over. Precious had promised to drop Jennie and Linda off at the mall on their way home. Pretty sat in the front seat of the car with her sister, quietly angry with herself for not bringing her own car. She wanted to fly home after her encounter with Malcolm. Linda was so excited; this was the first time that the women came away with more telephone numbers than the men did, and she and Jennie were comparing the telephone numbers they had received. They both had four numbers; ironically, neither had one number alike. Precious, for some reason, didn't speak about any telephone numbers that she had received at the brunch. Linda then touched Pretty on her shoulder and asked how many numbers she had received. Pretty answered somewhat sarcastically, "I did not seek any telephone numbers, my dear." Precious chuckled hearing her sister's answer, she couldn't wait for the girls to get out of the car. Precious then said, "Ladies, don't spend too much money." They replied, "Thank you," gave her a kiss, and got out of the car.

Pretty knew that Precious was ready to talk, however, she had already decided she was not going to talk about it at all. "OK. Ms. Tough Girl, what happened to you back there?" said Precious. "What are you talking about?" said Pretty. "You know what I'm talking about, I know you very well, sis." "What do you mean?" replied Pretty. "Do I really need to spell it out? Malcolm, what happened? I have never seen you buckled under before." Pretty turned her head and stared out the window. "Nothing happened, I think I ate something that didn't agree with me," she replied. "Sure," said Precious, "I'll let you absorb what happened to you, but we'll talk later." Pretty was so happy that her sister was not pushing the issue. She herself didn't totally understand what had happened to her. The girls arrived at their home. Pretty quietly got out of the car, went into the house, straight to her room, and closed the door.

Pretty threw herself on the bed, face down. Every time she attempted to reflect on her meeting with Malcolm her stomach would start to quiver. She wasn't sure what was happening to her. Something inside her wanted to think about it, but each time she did, she would have a feeling of fear and anxiety all rolled into one. She wanted to look at Malcolm's telephone number, but just thinking about it, she would start to shake and break out into a cold sweat. After trying to think about him, Pretty just jumped up, ran into the bathroom, and started throwing cold water on her face. She looked into the mirror at herself and asked, *what is happening to me?* She had finally met someone that she was attracted to she could not believe it. He seemed to be someone that may have the qualities that she believed she was looking for in a man; she, however, wasn't sure about anything at that moment. Pretty had decided to take her clothes off and get into the shower; she thought it would make her feel better. She wasn't in any pain; she just didn't know what to do with herself, so she showered and took a nap, at three o'clock in the afternoon.

While Pretty was taking a nap, Precious was speaking with her mother about what had happened earlier that day. Penene was amused but not surprised. Penene told Precious that's usually how it happens; the one that appears very brave and chats the most about a man is the one that buckles first when confronted by a man. Penene then said, "I just pray that this Malcolm is the right man for her; it's time for her to meet someone nice that she could settle down with." Precious then said, "Mom, why are you marrying Pretty off so fast?" Penene then said, "Honey, Pretty is getting old and she needs a man in her life. She's not like you and Princess: you girls have had boyfriends and plenty of male friends. Pretty on the other hand has run every man away from her, so it's time for her to enjoy the opposite sex." "I see what you mean," said Precious. "I'm sure she is feeling a bit embarrassed so I'll go talk with her," said Penene.

Penene knocked a few times on Pretty's door and there was no answer, so she slowly opened the door. The room was very dark, so Penene called her name as she clicked on her lamp. Penene found her daughter sitting on a chair gazing out of a darkened window. "Hey baby, how are you?" said Penene. Pretty looked at her mom with tears in her eyes and her mother just reached out and hugged her. "What's wrong, baby?" "Mom, I don't know how I'm going back to work tomorrow. I know Precious told you what happened today, this man works at my job, what will I do? I don't know what to do, Mom, I don't know." Penene had a way of making all of her girls feel better when they were having a personal crisis, and she knew she had to do something for Pretty at this time.

"I heard you met a man today, love. Did this man do something to harm you, or do you feel threatened in some way?" No, mother," replied Pretty. "He did nothing but charm the heck out of me." Penene laughed. "Well dear, if that is all he did, embrace it and enjoy every minute of it. It's about time that you start dating and think about settling down, get to know him." "The funniest thing," said Pretty, "something inside of me feels as if I knew him all my life and I just met him. I don't know anything about him except for his name and where he came from. How is that possible?" "Anything is possible, sweetheart," said Panene. "Did you give him your telephone number?" "No way, he gave me his number," said Pretty. "I have to go to work tomorrow and he works on my job. How am I going to handle that?" "Did you ever see him before today?" said Panene. "I don't think so, but he has seen me, that's for sure." Well, honey, I think you should carry on as usual. Don't call him right away, maybe wait a few days until you calm down, and then take it from there." Pretty agreed with her mom and decided to take her advice. Penene then suggested that she talk with her sister because she was very concerned about her. She kissed Pretty on the cheek and left the room.

Precious poked her head into Pretty's room, and asked if she could come in. Pretty told her, "Yes, come on in." Precious then said to her sister, "You had a long nap. Are you feeling better now?" "I'm not really sure how I'm feeling right now; I've never felt this way before." "What do you mean?" replied Precious. "I met Malcolm and somehow it feels like I have known him all my life," said Pretty. "I'm nervous but I still feel a bit calm, I can't explain it." "You don't have to explain it," said Precious. "It's called love at first sight, it really happens, you know. We have read so many stories of couples who met, just looked at each other for the first time, and they have been married for forty years." Pretty started to laugh, saying, "Are you marrying me off, sis?" "Well, this is the first time meeting a man ever done this to you, so you never know. Plus the way he looked at you, I felt something, it was so real and intense," said Precious. "Yes, I felt it also," said Pretty. "Well, I'm going to take it slow, one day at a time," she said. Precious then started to look somewhat excited: "Maybe this is the beginning of your love story, Pretty." "I can't wait for the beginning of your love story," said Pretty, "I can't wait." "Me either," said Precious. "We seem to be going in age order, so I guess I am next." The two sisters then had a good laugh together.

The next day Pretty was a bit nervous; however, she put on her brave face and left for work as usual. The entire day went by and she did not see Malcolm, though she did look for him slightly. At the end of the day she packed for the gym, her friend Gwen came by, and everything was normal. Pretty just knew Gwen would mention something about her and Malcolm, but to her surprise, Gwen did not mention a thing. She did mention Malcolm's friend Chauncey and another fellow named Tyrone. Gwen had received both their telephone numbers, and she wasn't sure which one she really wanted to call. A week had passed and Gwen still never mentioned Malcolm, nor did Pretty see him. Gwen had decided to talk to Tyrone; that was a relief for Pretty. There was little chance of Gwen bringing up Malcolm in conversation; and she realized Gwen did not really know what had happened at the brunch.

Two weeks had passed by and Precious was bugging Pretty about calling Malcolm, but Pretty was not ready to call him. On the third week, Monday afternoon at approximately three thirty, Pretty was preparing to go home. She wasn't going to the gym this day and her friend Gwen didn't come to work. As Pretty was about to leave the room, she turned to grab her bag and there he was, Malcolm, standing in her doorway with the most beautifully warm smile. For an instant she got nervous, but time had eased her nervousness somewhat. She was actually looking forward to seeing him and talking with him. In a strong and manly voice Malcolm said, "Good afternoon, pretty lady." Pretty smiled back and said, "Good afternoon to you, sir." He then said, "I was waiting for your call, but I figured you lost my number so I decided to give you another chance." "You did, did you"? she replied. They both smiled at each other and Malcolm then said to her, "How about dinner tonight?" Pretty answered, "Yes, why not?" and the rest was history.

Malcolm and Pretty had become an item after three months. Malcolm appeared to be everything Pretty wanted in a man; he was strong and manly and he could really handle her. When she started to talk rough, he would calm her right down; she loved every minute of him. She also was the perfect woman for him; she knew how to keep him balanced. He was twenty-nine years old, never married, once engaged, with no children, a teacher/administrator who had just received his assistant principal license and wanted to settle down and have a family. He had moved to the suburbs from New York City after a broken engagement, one he never talked about, nor did Pretty ask any questions. Malcolm wanted a change and a slower pace, to have a family and raise children. He was also trying to be very cautious when it came to women. It was obvious he had had a bad experience with his previous engagement, and he did not want to repeat the experience. Pretty loved the fact that he was religious and had values and morals; he was just perfect so far. She still wondered about 'you know what'.

It was approximately one year later and Patrick and Penene was preparing for their annual family barbeque. The Wednesday before the barbeque Malcolm had landed the assistant principal position in another school, a position he had applied for six months earlier. Pretty had decided to surprise Malcolm with a cake and a briefcase to celebrate his accomplishment. What she didn't know was that he was planning to surprise her with an engagement ring. Patrick, Panene, Princess, King, and Precious all knew about the surprises and they managed to keep both secrets.

At the barbeque Pretty revealed her surprise first, and Malcolm was truly surprised. As he was making his thank-you speech, he looked over at Pretty and said, "This has been an incredible year for me. I found a comfortable place to live and settle down, I landed the job I always wanted, and finally I found the perfect woman to settle down with." With that he walked over to Pretty, pulled a one-carat pink diamond ring out of his pocket, got down on one knee and said, "Pretty, I have your father and mother's permission and now I ask you, will you marry me?" This was the second time Pretty was ever speechless. She was ecstatically surprised; she started crying and said, "Yes, Malcolm Henry, I will marry you." The family started to congratulate the couple, and most of the women went to look at Pretty's ring. Across the yard, her uncle Cadillac looked directly at her aunt Shelly, and Shelly quickly turned her head and went to look at her nieces' ring.

That night Pretty insisted on going home with Malcolm; she

was still excited from the day. He just wanted to go home and rest from the activities of the day. However, he knew she was excited and wanted to be with him alone for a while, just to enjoy the engagement moment. When they got to his house, Malcolm was so tired that he went into his bedroom to hang up his clothes, and the next thing you know he was laying across his bed. He was so quiet for so long that Pretty went to see what he was doing; she found him fast asleep, and she just looked at her husband-to-be and smiled.

Pretty began thinking about her conversation with Malcolm earlier in their relationship. She had told him she was a virgin and had made a pact with her sisters to remain one until she was married, and he agreed she should. She had also discussed her theory on sex before marriage. Malcolm never agreed or disagreed; he would just listen to her talk about it. Pretty had tried so many times before to get him to touch her in a sexual manner but he would never do it. She oftentimes thought he was bisexual or something because he never really showed any interest sexually. He was very affectionate with her all the time but he would never make sexual advances. He would kiss her passionately, hug and even rub her, but only her back or her arms, always staying a perfect gentleman. A little too perfect, she thought. She could not understand why he would not make sexual advances toward her. He wasn't a virgin, and she knew that even though they never spoke about it.

As Malcolm lay sleeping, Pretty went to the bathroom, slipped off her clothes, and got into the shower. She came out the shower with a towel wrapped around her, took a deep breath, pulled off Malcolm's pants and shirt, and got in the bed next to him. Tonight was her night; she wanted to test the waters, and she was ready. Her heart was beating so fast, but she felt brave and determined. This night she did not care about the pact she and her sisters made; in her mind this was her husband-to-be and it would be all right to have sex with him. Plus, her theory was to have sex before marriage so you wouldn't be stuck with a lemon.

Pretty just knew that Malcolm would not be a lemon, because she loved him, and she wanted all of him this night. Her hands were sweating and her heart was beating fast, but she wanted to experience all the things she had heard about in her sister's dreams of love, and she was ready.

Pretty began to rub her hands over his entire property, from the roof to the ground floor. As she reached the midfloor, there her man was standing at attention, straight as a soldier saluting her. Pretty was startled and her body started ticking like a bomb. She didn't know what to do next; this time her inner thighs were on fire, burning with a passion she had never felt before. Everything in her said this was what she wanted tonight. Suddenly Malcolm pulled her close to him and her body trembled even more. Pretty held on tight and began to kiss his chest as not to look up but for him to keep going. His passion was aroused and he kissed her face hard and passionately and down to her breast, each one gently and firm. This was the very first time that she had ever felt this way with him. Pretty was ready.

As Malcolm almost entered the door to her world, he awoke. When he realized what was happening he jumped up with the sheet wrapped around him, exclaiming, "What are you doing Pretty, are you crazy?" Pretty shouted out, "Malcolm, I'm ready, please I'm ready baby, take me." He yelled back from the bathroom as he was putting on his underwear, "No baby, you are not ready. You promised to save yourself and that's what you need to do." Pretty got angry, and she went to the bathroom behind him shouting, "This is my body, my virginity, can't I make my own decisions?" "Yes baby, you can, but this is not the time." Pretty wrapped her arms around Malcolm's neck and started kissing him on the neck, whispering, "I know you want me, I can feel you when I touch you, please baby, you can have me now, I'm ready." He pushed her off and pulled his robe off the door, saying, "Please, put on some clothes, this is not the time." She followed him to the bedroom, to the living room, naked and begging, "What is wrong with you, are you gay or something? Why don't you want me? You want to marry me but you don't want to have sex with me." Pretty sat down on a chair and started to cry. Malcolm brought her clothes and draped her blouse over her shoulder, saying, "Please get dressed, honey, I think you should go home and rest; we'll talk about this tomorrow." "I don't want to talk tomorrow, Malcolm, I want you to make love to me or you can forget the engagement. I don't want to marry a man that's gay, I knew it was to good to be true, you're gay, aren't you?" said Pretty. Malcolm grabbed her two arms and stood her up, in a strong masculine voice and with a confident look in his eyes, he said, "No sweetheart, I'm not gay, or bisexual. I'm very much a man and you will get to know that soon enough, but not now." Pretty stood for a minute, looked at Malcolm, and went to the bedroom and got dressed. When she returned Malcolm was sitting quietly. Pretty took off her engagement ring, placed it on the table in front of him, and said, "Good-bye, Malcolm."

Malcolm jumped up, blocked the door, and said, "You will not leave this way, so sit down, let's talk." "I have nothing to say," said Pretty. "Let me leave." Malcolm then led her to the couch and pushed her gently to sit down. "You do not have to say anything; I will do the talking this time and you will listen," he said. "I never spoke about my previous engagement to you, but I think it's time I did." Pretty said in a harsh tone, "You do not have to tell me about your previous love stories, I am not interested." "Pretty, close your mouth for once and listen," said Malcolm.

"I met this beautiful girl named Denise; she was everything I thought I wanted. We went out for about two months. I found out she wasn't a virgin; she had been with two guys before me. I was a bit concerned in the beginning; however, I did not let that worry me. We had decided to take physicals and blood tests before we would get intimate, and we did. Soon after, we were intimate and all was well. After approximately six months, we were engaged; all was still well. We had picked a date for the wedding and everything, but about two months later things started to change. Denise did not act the same, the sex wasn't the same, nothing was the same. The respect she had for me disappeared, everything was different. Then I realized what had happened: we dated for approximately, two months and then we were intimate. We did not even fall in love with each other; we were in lust with each other, and that had begun to fade away. Everything went downhill from there. After one year or so we found out we really did not like the same things or each other. We were only comfortable in bed; out of bed, we had become enemies. Then we waited to see which one of us would break the engagement first. Naturally, neither one of us wanted to be first to break up, we both were too proud for it to be our fault. Following was another six months of misery, the lust we had for each other was gone; we had nothing but bitterness. Finally, Denise started sleeping with someone else and set it up for me to find out. The nightmare engagement was finally over.

"Pretty, I realized so many things from that experience. The advice my parents gave to my sister and I was true. 'Fall in love first, children, and you will enjoy everything about the person that you fell in love with.' I tried it my way and it didn't work. I realized any two people could fall in lust with each other, but I wanted the one I could fall in love with first. I believe that would be somewhat of a guarantee that a marriage will have a better chance at lasting. I now realize that is true, especially since I met and fell in love with you, no lust involved, just you. When I moved out here, I came on a mission, a mission to do things differently. I was very determined to find the love of my life, to fall in love, not lust. I could fall in lust a hundred times a day. That isn't what I want, it's superficial.

"When I saw you for the first time sitting at your desk, I knew I wanted to get to know you. Then I heard you speak and I thought to myself, what a beautiful challenge. I watched you walk, and the way you carried yourself just lit up my heart and I had to know you. You would never smile at me, but you would smile at others. Your smile, everything about you just made me want you even more. My body yearned for you but I wanted to fall in love with you, not lust for you first. Then I finally met you and that's when I knew, I knew it as soon as I spoke with you and you answered me back. I said to Chauncey, "That is going to be my wife, the mother of my children; I found her, my soul mate." Yes, Chauncey thought I was crazy, but I knew I wasn't.

"Pretty, I love you; I love the fact that you are a virgin. I did not want to make love to you and fall in lust with you, that would have been too easy. I wanted to fall in love with you. I knew I would love everything about you." Pretty then said, "So what is the problem, you fell in love first and now. ..." Malcolm took Pretty's two hands into his, looked into her eyes, and said, "Sweetie, if we waited this long, why not wait a little bit longer? Let's leave something for our imagination, and let me respect you. What will we have new to try if we do everything now? Just think about it, on our honeymoon night we get to explore something new about each other, and believe me, I know we are going to be great together. Ask your sister Princess, would she have done it any other way? Pretty, you are worth the wait to me, and you deserve it. Let me love you the right way honey, not lust for you. You waited this long, because you deserve that."

Then Malcolm picked up the ring and said to her, "Ms. Pretty, again I ask, will you marry me?" Pretty looked into his eyes in tears and said, "Yes, Malcolm Henry, again I will marry you. On one condition." "What is that?" said Malcolm. "That we don't have a long engagement." Malcolm looked at her and they both smiled; he then grabbed her close to him and squeezed her very hard. Pretty could feel his manhood close to her and her stomach started to flutter. Malcolm then said, "Pretty, in time you will find out that I'm not gay," and he pushed her away from him and said, "Now go home.

8. Tricks of Love
(A P in a Pod)
Part One

Precious was attending a mandatory training for elementary school teachers; it was the beginning of the school year. As she packed her bag to leave the training, a handsome man walked over to her with a smile on his face, Precious smiled back as he approached. He said, "Good afternoon, my name is Neville," and he stuck his hand out to shake hers. Precious shook his hand and told him her name. "Did you get anything from this class?" he asked. "Yes, I did receive some helpful information and what about you?" she said. "Yes, I thought it to be pretty resourceful. Where do you teach?" he asked. Precious answered his questions with a smile. Neville looked straight into her eyes and said to her, "You are the most beautiful woman I've seen in quite a long time. How do you stay so beautiful?" At the same time he took her bag out of her hand to carry it. Precious was flattered by his manners, and she started to blush. Neville then asked if she would like to go out sometime, to dinner or a play or something. Precious said, "That sounds fine; I would like that." Something about him attracted her; he was smooth talking and very much a gentleman. He carried bags, opened doors, and was very protective of her.

Precious was intrigued with that type of behavior in a man. He walked her to her car and they exchanged telephone numbers.

On the drive home, Precious was daydreaming about Neville, who really left an impression on her. Something about him was interesting, but something else was telling her to be a bit cautious. Not cautious like she would be in danger, but something else that she could not figure out yet. Precious started thinking how Princess was happily married and Pretty was engaged; was it time for her? She didn't want to be hasty, because she had just met him, and there was something about him that stayed on her mind. As she drove up into her driveway, her telephone rang. When she answered it, it was Neville; she could not believe it. In a smooth soothing voice, he said, "Hi there, I'm sorry, I just had to call you, I couldn't stop thinking about you." Precious just smiled; she didn't say anything right away. Neville then said, "Hello, did you hear me?" "Yes I did," answered Precious. "I heard you." She then asked if she could call him back because she had just gotten home, and he said sure. Precious thought she was very smart when it came to men and affairs, so she had decided she wasn't going to call him back right away. However, something inside of her really wanted to call him back right away and stay on the telephone with him all night.

When Precious got into the house, her mom and sister were sitting in the living room looking through magazines at wedding dresses. Pretty looked up and said, "Come on, Precious, tell me what dress you like, what could you see me in." Precious came right over to the couch and started looking through the pictures. She was looking but her mind was on Neville; she could not stop thinking about this man. Pretty then asked Precious, "How was the training, anything interesting?" "Yes, it was resourceful; I actually enjoyed it, for the first time." "That's good," said Pretty. Then Precious's telephone rang. She looked at the number and then excused herself from her sister and mom and went into her room; it was Neville again. Penene and Pretty looked at each other. They thought it was a bit strange, but Precious always did strange things, so they didn't really think much of it. They quickly resumed looking through the magazines.

Precious went into her room and flopped on the bed. "Girl, I don't know what you did to me, but I can't get you out of my head," said Neville. "I just want to hear your voice all day and night." Precious started blushing and smiling, she answered back finally, "Really?" That was all she could say. As the night went on, Neville and Precious spoke for about three hours, they started out talking about work and then some of everything. Pretty knocked on Precious's door and then opened it like the sisters always did, but she found her sister on the telephone so she left her alone.

The next morning, Precious was on the telephone early, before she even showered for work. She and Neville had been talking all night and they started again early in the morning. Pretty came into Precious's room and found her sister on the telephone again. This time Pretty waited for her to hang up. "What man did you meet, when, where, how and most important, who is he?" "Oh Pretty, what makes you think it's a man?" Precious said, "You're talking to me, your sister. I know it's a man, now who is he?" "He's really nobody, just a man I met at the training yesterday," said Precious. Pretty shouted, "Yesterday and you're talking to him like that already? I thought you knew him forever the way you were talking on the telephone. When are we going to meet him?" "Slow down Pretty, not so fast, I just met him; I don't know if I'm ready to bring him home." "Well, if you are talking to him day and night, I think you need to consider it. What is his name?" "Neville," replied Precious. "Neville what, from where?" said Pretty. Precious stopped for a minute, and then she said, "I don't even know, I never asked, we talked about so many things. Oh well, I guess we have even more to talk about now." "I've never seen you like this, Precious, be careful, and I hope you know what you're doing." "I'm not doing anything, Pretty, and I'm always careful. You're talking to me."

When the workday was over Precious was on the telephone all the way home. When she got home, Penene greeted her at the door; she was on her way out to a meeting. As she passed Precious she said, "I sure want to meet this guy that has your attention this past day and a half." Precious kissed her mom and went in the house. She went straight to her room laid on the bed with the telephone in her ear. Talking with Neville, she found out that he was not a teacher. His name was Neville George, he was in a teaching program, and he wasn't sure if he wanted to become a teacher or not. He was interested in music, writing, and playing the keyboard, which seemed to be his real passion. Precious found that part of his life interesting because writing love stories was very similar to writing lyrics for songs. However, she did not tell him that she wrote stories; it was still very personal for her.

That evening Pretty came home and called out for Precious, she wanted to share some news with her. Precious told Neville that she would have to speak with him later, after dinner. He wanted to know why she had to hang up. Couldn't her sister wait? He needed to talk with her some more. Pretty then came into the room. "Precious, Precious, I have something to tell you, hang up for a minute." Precious was still trying to convince Neville that she would call him back; finally, he agreed, but he seemed a bit angry. Pretty stopped for a moment and said, "What's up with him? You just met him yesterday." "Oh, he's all right, he's just having some issues right now and I seem to be helping him through them," said Precious. "That is still pretty quick for a new friendship; please, I hope you know what you're doing, sis. When will we met this Neville anyway?" said Pretty. "Soon, don't worry, soon, I promise," replied Precious.

Pretty then, very excited, said, "Guess where I booked for the wedding reception, guess." "Where?" said Precious. "Where?" "The ballroom at the big Plaza Hotel, it is so beautiful." "Wow," said Precious. "It must be expensive." "Not too bad, a couple of thousand, plus Malcolm insisted on paying for part of the wedding, and I accepted. He said he's only getting married once, and I figured I could save mom and dad some money. They still have your wedding to pay for," and she then laughed. Precious was excited but not really for herself.

She seemed to be in a quiet hurry, and Pretty recognized that she wanted to get back to the telephone. So she said to her, "I'm going over to Malcolm's to give him the good news. Do you want to go for the ride?" "No thanks, I have some work I need to complete for my students tomorrow. You go ahead, I'll talk with you later," said Precious. Pretty was worried about her sister but she left to give Malcolm the news. On the way to his house she telephoned her mother to give her the news and to mention Precious's peculiar behavior.

As Pretty left, Precious's telephone rang. It was Neville; this time he wanted to take her out to dinner, and she accepted. While she was getting ready to leave the house, her mother was coming in. "Hey baby, where are you going?" said Penene. "I'm going out to dinner with a friend, mom, I'll be back later." "Is this your new mystery friend?" said her mother. "Mother, he's not a mystery, his name is Neville George." "When will we meet him? You're going out with someone that no one in your family has ever seen. That's not good, Precious. How much do you really know about this fellow?" "Mom, what's the problem, you've never questioned any of us like this before." "Well, none of you ever acted so secretive before; someone in your family or circle of friends always knew or seen the person that you were going out with." Patrick then came in from work and asked what was going on. Panene explained the conversation to him. Patrick was a very calm yet stern father, and he had much respect for his grown daughters. He turned to his wife and asked her to leave him and Precious alone for a minute. Panene walked off a bit disturbed, but she had confidence that her husband would handle the situation.

Patrick then asked his daughter if she was all right; she told him that she was fine. Patrick then said to her, "Listen baby: in light of the times we're living in, I think it's a wise thing to have your friend pick you up for dinner. This way we get to see his face and his car. Not that anything is going to happen to you, plus I respect the fact that you are grown, but just in case his face is on *America's Most Wanted,* I could identify him." He pinched her on the cheek like a little girl and laughed. "Not to mention your mother would sleep tonight and not keep me up. I had a long day, what do you say?" Precious looked at her father's smile and said, "You won, daddy. I'll call him and tell him to pick me up." Precious went to call Neville and Patrick went to talk to his wife. After Patrick told Penene the arrangements, she called Pretty to inform her that this man was coming over to pick her sister up tonight.

When Precious called Neville and asked that he pick her up so she would not have to drive, he was reluctant. He told her that he was going to meet her at the restaurant because he was on the other side of town, and if he picked her up he would still have to take her home and get back home. He explained that they both had work tomorrow and that would cut their time in the restaurant. Precious didn't really understand what the problem was, and then Neville said to her, why don't you drive, then you can pick me up? Precious then said to him, "Listen, I really want you to pick me up so that you can meet my family." "Meet your family, why tonight? I just want to go out to dinner with you, baby, not your family." "I can't explain it now but it would be better for me if you met them. They won't go to dinner with us. They think I'm talking to a mystery man and I want them to meet you." "Why tonight, Precious?" They went back and forth until Neville convinced her that they would go out another night when they had more time and he was more prepared to meet her folks. He also told her that they had just met and he felt that she was moving very fast in wanting him to meet her family. He convinced her that they should get to know one another a little bit longer before they take that step. Precious was disappointed- but he convinced her to understand what he was talking about, and the dinner was off.

Precious did not know how to tell her parents what had happened, so she decided to tell a small lie. She was uncomfortable not being honest with them, but she felt she was grown and she should not have to explain her business. She was not fifteen years old, plus she was embarrassed. She went into the kitchen and her father and mother were eating. "What's for dinner, mom?" she said. "I thought you were going out for dinner, honey," said Panene. "I changed my mind," said Precious. "It's pretty late to go out for dinner and we both have work tomorrow. I just asked him for a rain check and I figured I'd either invite him over to meet you guys or something. I don't really know if he's someone I want to meet my family yet. I don't even know if it's going to be a long relationship or not." She was talking so much and so fast that her father and mother just looked at her while she was preparing a plate of food. When she finished fixing her plate, she excused herself and went to eat in her room. Patrick and Panene looked at each other shocked. Panene said, "What the hell was that? Who was that?" Patrick just shook his head: "I don't know, I really don't know, but I don't think I like this Neville person; he doesn't have a good effect on my baby girl."

Precious went to her room with her food, and she was feeling very uncomfortable about lying to her parents. Something inside of her wanted to call Neville, but she was angry with him. She wanted everything to be smooth, but still deep down inside she had a funny feeling about him, a feeling that she couldn't explain or put her finger on. She ate her food and did not call him, nor did he call her. Precious had in her mind to write but she drifted off to sleep. As she drifted to sleep she started to dream; this time her characters had faces and familiar names, which was unusual.

There she was standing in the mirror putting on her white mink coat with a wide white mink hat, nothing underneath but a pure white teddy with a lace bodice. She stopped to pull up her white fishnet stockings with a white garter holding them up. She then looked around to see what shoes or boots she would put on; she decided to wear the white short turned-down pointed-toe boots. She looked at her completed project, twirled around, and smiled. Suddenly a rush of butterflies flooded her stomach; she took a deep breath, fastened her coat, and off she went to meet her husband. On the way out the door, she grabbed the bottle of wine she had picked up earlier. Today was her one-month anniversary, and she wanted to surprise him; she wanted to show him how much she had learned in one month.

You see, she had listened to some of his stories of previous encounters with women, and she wanted him to want her always, so she decided to be adventurous and try something worldly. Nervous wasn't the word for her; as she got closer and closer to his office she felt like a ton of lead was holding her back, but she knew she couldn't stop. She decided to call him to make sure he was alone in the office. "Hi baby, are you free?" she asked. "Yes, love, trying to get home to you." "Honey, I was in the neighborhood dropping something off to my sister, so I'm going to stop by." "That's fine, love; I'll be waiting for you." When she hung up, she felt like a virgin all over again, as if it was the first time she was going to be with her husband. She stopped the car in front of his office and just sat there for a moment. She thought, maybe he might think I'm crazy to dress like this tonight, or maybe he may get angry with me. Her mind just started racing. She lifted her head, looked into the car mirror and said to herself, Be brave, you can do this, *and she got out of the car and grabbed the bottle of wine.*

As she approached his office building, she bravely walked right in the door. She opened it and locked it behind her. She then yelled out to her husband; when he came out there, she was standing there with her coat slightly open, wine in hand and a smile on her face. "Happy one-month anniversary," she said. Neville stood there, looking at his wife in shock and speechless. Precious walked up to him, put her arms around his neck, and started passionately kissing him on his neck and his face until she slipped his arm out of his jacket and started unbuttoning his shirt. Precious backed her husband to the couch and down he went. Neville stopped her for a moment and said, "Who are you and where is my wife?" She laughed and continued to kiss him passionately. Suddenly, he was not the same person anymore. He had become a super lover; everything about him changed. He became strong and forceful but gentle, and his face changed from that of a smooth handsome husband to a serious, focused lover. When she observed the change in his every part, nervousness came over her, one that she could not explain; it was scary and somewhat frightening.

As he began to undress his furry soft creature, it was as if someone had given her a tranquilizer. She could not move her hands or lips in the manner that she had done before; they froze. Her body, however, started to shake like an earthquake, uncontrollably. A fire had ignited in her that consumed her from within. As the fire had her in a passionate heat, all he did was look at her and put his hands on her upper extremities and the water just poured from her body like a hose turned on inside of her. Her lover felt boastfully confident, he was at ease to know that his job was half done, that fire wasn't that uncontrollable for him, he had the power over this beautiful little creature. Then he slowly, but bravely, began to enter the remaining flames. ... Then there was a loud crash; it was Precious's dinner plate hitting the floor. When she fully awoke, she was soaking wet with sweat. Precious jumped up hot and sweaty with an uneasy feeling inside. This was the first time that she had ever had one of her dreams with an uneasy feeling afterward. She did not want to pay much attention to it either. All she could think about was Neville in her dreams as her husband. Precious looked at the time, went to take a shower, and off to bed she went.

9. Tricks of Love ... This Is Not a Dream
Part Two

It was the end of September: school had just started again, Pretty was engaged to Malcolm and they had picked a wedding date in February. Pretty wanted a short engagement and Malcolm wanted a winter wedding, so they both were happy with the date. Panene had planned a formal engagement party for the two; she wanted the two families to have the opportunity to meet before the actual wedding. Pretty had met Malcolm's parents last year; he also had one sister whom she had never met. She had spoken to her several times on the telephone. She would not make it for the dinner, but she would make the wedding. The family was buzzing with Pretty's wedding plans. The engagement party was scheduled for October, the Columbus Day weekend; Penene figured most people were off that weekend and it would be most convenient for everyone.

A few weeks had passed and Precious was still talking with Neville on the telephone every chance she got. She still had not gone out to dinner with him, however, he did come to her job and take her out for lunch twice. He was definitely a charmer, one with a few issues of concern. He had not decided what he wanted to do with his career yet, but he was in some local educational program. He was living with a roommate who he said was a female, and they were having some issues with the bills or something. His biggest thing was he was not speaking to his father, so he wouldn't even call his mother. Precious felt a little sorry for him because he would always seem sad when he spoke about his parents.

It was one week before the engagement party and Penene was constantly preparing. Unlike Princess's engagement, Penene had Princess, Pretty, and Precious's help, nevertheless, things were different this time. Princess was married and did not live at home, so she wasn't there every day. Pretty was busy at work and taking care of other things for the wedding. Last, Precious was so preoccupied with her new friend, whom no one had seen yet, that she wasn't much help to anyone. Thankfully, it wasn't a large party, just for the immediate family. It was for Malcolm's parents, a "get acquainted before the actual wedding" dinner party. Penene thought it would be a good idea, considering his parents did not live in the area.

Now it was three days before the party, and the three, Penene, Princess and Pretty was doing some last-minute things. They started to discuss Precious. Penene explained how she was very concerned about the entire situation, because Precious's behavior lately had not been normal. Pretty agreed and said that she had tried to talk with Precious about this Neville person and she became very defensive. Princess then stated that they should give it some time; Precious was a very intelligent individual. She believed she would be very cautious, and she asked, "Don't you agree?" Pretty said she was not sure what Neville could influence her to do or not do. "Come on now, slow down, Pretty," said Princess. "She just met this man. You both are failing to realize that Precious might be going through some things herself. Precious is so full of love, and always looking for love. Look at her life now: I'm married and moved out; hard girl Pretty is engaged and getting married soon. She will be left home alone, still looking for love.

I'm sure she must be going through some feelings now," said Princess. "That's what I'm worried about," said Penene. "She's vulnerable right now and this Neville might be taking advantage of the situation and possibly of her."

At that moment, Patrick walked into the room and said, "Yes, ladies, I heard all three of you and I think Princess might be right. I think we need to leave Precious alone for a while and give her some time to come to us about this new guy in her life. She has always been the type to figure out things on her own and only then would she talk about it. So promise me, ladies, you won't put any pressure on her right now; just keep your eyes and ears open and let's not push her away. The most important thing to remember is she isn't a little girl any more. You, Princess, have entered another world and Pretty, you are about to embark on a new world come February. Precious is the last now, and I'm sure it must be hard on her not having the support of her sisters as close as it was. She realizes that you girls have and will enter that world of love that she so desperately wants for herself."

As Patrick was ending his statement, they heard a key in the door. It was Precious. "Good evening, everyone, what's going on?" said Precious. Princess went over and gave her a big hug and kiss, saying, "Hey sis, I miss you, how are you?" "I'm good. Are you guys finished with everything? Can I help with something, mom?" "No, baby, we're finished, thanks," said Penene. "I'm sorry, I got caught up with my friend, he's going though some things right now, it's amazing that some people have so many issues, we are so blessed." Then Precious turned to Pretty and said, "Are you getting nervous yet?" then kissed her on the cheek. Pretty just pushed Precious away from her, and they all started to laugh. Penene then said, "Well, just think, in approximately one year you'll probably be getting married too." "Then your father and I will start turning your rooms into hobby rooms or bedrooms for our grandchildren,". Patrick then yelled into the kitchen, "No more children in this house unless its boys, I mean that." "Sure, dad, that's what you say now," said Pretty. Pretty then went into her room, and Princess followed. Precious's telephone rang, and she went into her own room.

A few minutes later Precious came into Pretty's room; they were sitting on the floor talking. "What are you girls talking about, sex or marriage?" said Precious "Nothing, being tired and work. How is your job going this year?" said Princess. "Everything is good so far. Did mom and Pretty tell you I met a man?" said Precious. Pretty then said, "Do you think I have time to tell Princess what you're doing while I'm running around making wedding plans? Anyway, you just met him. You're not even sure how you feel about him, are you?" said Pretty. "Wow, I'm really missing a lot not being here, aren't I?" said Princess. You're not missing a thing big sister, trust me, it's the same old thing, said Precious.

Princess then said, well tell me all about this new guy, what's his name, what's he like?" Precious laid back with her head resting on a chair: "His name is Neville George, and so far, I think he's all right. I don't really know much about him as yet, but I enjoy being in his company." "Did you meet him at work?" said Princess. "No, I met him at a mandatory teachers training." "Oh, he's a teacher?" said Princess. "No, not really, it's a bit complicated; I'll explain that to you another time, it'll take too long." Pretty then said, "Hey, why don't you bring him to the engagement party? It might be nice for you and him." "Thank you," said Precious. "I just might do that."

Princess then turned to Precious and asked, "What about those dreams, girl, how are they going?" All three girls started to laugh very hard, and then they started to reminisce. Precious said, "My dreams are a bit weird these days. I now have dreams with names and faces, but every time the man gets ready to complete his duties, I wake up. Ironically, the woman is satisfied before anything really happens. It's really strange; I have never had dreams like that before." Pretty then said, "I think you need a dream interrupter, girl. I cannot help you. All I know is I can't wait for that night; I definitely will let Malcolm do his duties."

Princess laughed. Then Pretty said, "I even tried to get him to do his duties before our 'I do's'. Princess and Precious both said, "What?" "You are a sick girl," said Princess, "sick." "I did," said Pretty, "and he refused all of this," motioning to her body. "I don't know how that man can stand you; he's either very brave or absolutely crazy," said Precious. Princess then got up off the floor and said, "It's time for me to go home to my husband. Ladies, I will probably see you people tomorrow. I'm going to tell mom and dad goodnight," and then she kissed her sisters.

Precious then said, "Good night, I have a long day tomorrow." As soon as she left Pretty's room, she picked up her telephone and called Neville. The telephone just rang and there was no answer. This was the first time he didn't answer her calls right away, so she decided to wait a few minutes and call back. As she started taking off her clothes, her phone rang. It was Neville. "I'm sorry; I was busy," said Neville. "That's fine," said Precious. Then she said, "Neville, I need you to do me a favor." "A favor?" said Neville. "Yes, I need a date for a dinner party on Sunday. Can you accompany me?" "A dinner party, what does that mean?" he said. "A dinner party, you know, sit down; have dinner, a little music, drinks and chats after the meal." "I don't think so," said Neville. "Come on, please, I need a date; I'll be the only one without a date." After Precious begged him for about ten minutes, he agreed. Then he asked where this dinner party would be, and she said it was with her sisters, but she never told him it was at her house with her parents. Precious then told Neville that she would call him right back, and hung up the telephone. She did not want him to ask any more questions about the dinner party; for some reason she knew he wouldn't want to go if he knew it was at her house with her parents.

As Precious was in her room, Pretty was talking to her mom about the conversation she and her sister had with Precious. Penene said, "Mark my words, that man will not be coming over here for dinner; he will have an excuse or she will make one for him." "We will see," said Pretty. ".I'm taking daddy's advice and I am not going to ask her anything about it or him. I will let her talk to me, and I'm trying to be more positive about it, even though I have a funny feeling about him. I am going to Google him and ask around about him. I would really like to know something about this character." "Yes, I would like to know also; keep me posted," said Penene. "And I'm going to bed."

The next day Neville and Precious met up as usual after work. They got some coffee and were sitting in his car. Neville told her that he was stressed out with his roommate and he was looking for a new apartment. He hadn't gotten any sleep over the past few days, because of her company and noise. For some reason in the back of Precious's mind she felt he was living with a woman in a bad relationship and they were breaking up, but she didn't have any proof, so she decided she would just listen to him talk. Precious asked him what he was going to do about the situation or how fast could he fix it. He wasn't really sure. He said he was exhausted and thinking about going to a hotel for a few days, just to get a good night's rest, but that wouldn't really solve his problem; it would only be a temporary fix. Precious told him, "Maybe you should consider it. Sometimes when you get proper rest you feel better about things and you can work through them with a clearer head." Neville thought that was a good idea; however, it would be costly and he needed to save his money for an apartment. Precious sat and thought for a minute, and when she looked over at him, he was dozing off. She felt so sorry for him; she just laid his head on her shoulder.

After fifteen minutes Neville awoke. Precious just looked at him; she was so sympathetic to his problem. She was very concerned about him, but she really wanted to talk about the dinner party. He never asked about the dinner party again, so she did not mention it. She wanted to tell him where it was but she didn't know how. She did not want to upset him and have him change his mind about coming altogether; after all, it was two days away. Neville then suggested that they get another cup of coffee and then they both needed to go home and get some rest. Precious agreed with him.

When he came back with the coffee, Precious had a suggestion for him: she could lend him the money for a hotel for the weekend and he could get some rest, and he could pay her back when he was in a better position. Neville just looked at her. "Why would you do that for me?" he asked. "You need some rest, and if you are having problems and I could help, why not?" Neville reached over, gave her a big hug, and said, "Thank you. I could really use the rest." Precious then said, "Besides, I want you well rested for the dinner party" and smiled. Neville just gave her a funny look and said, "You are slick, madam, aren't you?" He then proceeded to drive her to her car; before she got out she pulled her checkbook out of her pocketbook and started writing him a check. Precious said, "Would three hundred dollars be enough for the weekend?" and handed him the check. Neville shook his head yes and said, "I think it is more than enough; it would probably do for two weekends," and thanked her. As she was saying good night and had given him a kiss, he asked, "By the way, where is this dinner party going to be?" As she was getting out of his car and into hers, she shouted, "On Colonial Road," started her car, blew her horn, and drove off.

The next day Neville called early in the morning and asked Precious if she would go with him to check out a hotel he had found online. When she looked at the clock it was five thirty; she asked him what time he wanted her to come. He told her as soon as she could get ready. Of course Precious got right up and took a shower, and off she went to meet Neville at the Harrison Hotel, in the downtown area. Precious arrived before he did; he pulled up behind her about ten minutes later. They both got out of their cars and Neville kissed her rather hard on her lips. It was an unusual kiss, she thought. He was moving very fast, and she chalked it up to the anxiety of checking out the hotel and a lack of rest.

When they walked into the hotel, Precious thought he would ask questions about the place, but he didn't. He registered and received a key. Precious then asked him, "I thought you wanted to check this place out before you actually rented." "I checked it out online and I called after I spoke to you; that's why I was a little late. The price was right and I figured you could still check it out with me and give me your opinion." Precious did not understand his logic, nor did it make good sense, but she went along with it anyway. As she was going up the stairs with him, her telephone rang. It was Pretty. "Where are you? I thought you were in your room." "Oh, I had to go out this morning to help Neville," said Precious. "Is everything all right?" said Pretty. "Yes, thank you, I'm just checking out a hotel with him for the weekend." "A hotel for the weekend?" "Oh, I'll explain it to you when I see you," said Precious. Neville turned around and said, "Who are you telling my business to?" "This is my sister Pretty, it's OK." Precious then said, "Pretty, I'll call you back in a few minutes; did you want me for something?" Yes, did you forget we were going to help mom today with her final setup for tomorrow?" "I'll be home soon, I promise," said Precious.

They entered the room and Precious started walking around looking at everything. It was a very large room, a bedroom and living room combination. It looked very clean and it smelled nice. Neville went into the bathroom and when he came out, he was smiling. "How do you like it?" Precious said, "It looks very comfortable for a weekend or two. How is the price?" "The price is great; I can afford to use it for two weekends thanks to you." "That's great; you can finally get some rest."

Neville than laid on the bed and said, "This is comfortable; come feel it." "That's all right, thank you, I know how a bed feels," said Precious. Neville than got up and went over to Precious, he put his arms around her waist and started to kiss her. As she kissed him back, he began to kiss her passionately. Precious's heart started beating fast, and she wanted to push him away, but she could not. It was if she was under a spell or something. Neville started to rub her back in an up-and-down motion, straight down the middle of her back, and with every stroke, Precious's knees were buckling. As he rubbed her back, he kissed her neck from side to side until he came to her lips again. Neville slowly started kissing her down her chest, opening the top of her blouse with his teeth. His hands then gently came around to her breasts, cupping each one in his hands, and as he brought his lips to the tips of her perfectly formed mountains, Precious's knees gave way, falling right into Neville's arms. How his hands moved to catch her that fast was unbelievable. He picked her up and laid her on the bed; Precious had fainted. While she lay there on the bed, Neville undressed her from head to toe and put the sheet over her; he then undressed and got in the bed next to her.

Neville started to kiss Precious on her breasts and down her belly. At that moment she had regained consciousness but her eyes were closed tightly. Her body felt like it was on fire. He passionately rubbed his hands all over her, and when he touched between her legs there was a heat radiating from her like a furnace. Precious's eyes never opened as she laid there in ecstasy; she felt his tongue on her face and then on her neck, next down on each breast wetting them as he frantically moved from one to the other. She felt his wet tongue on her belly as she moved from side to side trying to get away. The feeling was overwhelming; she wanted to run, but his strong hands gripped her firmly and she could not move. As the wetness moved closer and closer down her thighs and up toward her treasures, she felt a wetness on her lower leg from his body and then a wetness in her forest at the same time. Neville's tongue had touched her upper gatekeeper; a frantic wetness then touched her lock. Precious's body had no control at this time. She moaned and sighed as she moved like a wild horse, bucking up and down trying to get away, but he grabbed her and laid his body hard on top of her, holding her hands tightly, trying to enter and unlock her treasures any way he could, using his legs to keep the gate open.

Suddenly, Precious realized she wasn't dreaming; it was real. She became very nervous, and she shouted, "Neville, what are you doing? Stop, I'm a virgin, stop!" However, she could not move her hands; he had them pinned back on the bed. She kept saying stop, stop but Neville paid no attention to her. All he said was "I know you are a virgin, don't worry, I'll be gentle, open up, baby." Precious had become frantic, and she said, "Neville, I'm going to scream. Please stop, I don't want it this way, please." "Scream baby, I like that, scream, come on Precious open up, I promise you'll enjoy every bit of it, open up," said Neville. Precious realized that this man was going to force her whether she wanted to or not, and she began to fight with everything in her. She used her legs to move him off her. When she finally got him off, she grabbed her pocketbook and ran into the bathroom. Neville just laid breathing hard. He then yelled out, "Why the hell are you here if you did not want to have sex?" Precious sat on the toilet crying; she didn't know what to do. She scrambled for her telephone in her bag, but she didn't know who to call; she was too embarrassed to call her family. Neville was still yelling and then he started banging on the door, "Come out of there, why did you come here?" Precious yelled back, "That's not why I came here." "Don't be so naive, Precious, why do you think I called you this early in the morning to come to a hotel with me?" Precious turned the water on. She could not stop crying; she threw some cold water on her face and looked in the mirror at herself. *You are so stupid, how are you going to get out of here with your clothes?* She sat back down on the toilet, and she heard Neville shouting again, "You have to come out sometime today. I'll wait, the room is paid for thanks to you" Precious looked at her telephone, and she thought, *call the police, but then they'll want to know why I'm here and how did my clothes get off.* She started to cry again. "I have to call somebody. Suddenly she thought, I know, call Malcolm, my brother-in-law to be, he's from New York City, I'm sure he'll know how to handle this situation and he'll be discreet."

Precious then fumbled to dial Malcolm's number, hoping that he answered; she was shaking, crying, and praying all at the same time. No answer, voice mail. She hung up and called again; this time he answered. Precious was crying and whispering, "Malcolm please I need your help, I'm at the Harrison hotel room 647 on the second floor, I'm trapped in the bathroom naked. Please, Neville is trying to rape me. Please don't call the police; please just come and get me. Please don't tell my parents, please," and she hung up. Malcolm never got a chance to say a word, nor would she have heard him anyway. Precious sat there crying and thinking about how this all had happened; she thought she was dreaming. She felt so stupid and embarrassed. How could she let this happen to her? She looked around in the bathroom, and she snatched down the shower curtain and wrapped it around her body like a dress, and then she started looking around for a weapon. She couldn't find anything in her pocketbook that she could use. *How dumb could I be?* she thought. Then she said to herself, m*aybe I should call my father. My father would kill this man.* Her mind was racing; she wanted to call her sisters, but she knew they would tell her parents. She was so confused; she just sat there and cried some more.

Precious did not realize how long she was sitting there; she was just numb. Then she heard a knock on the door, Neville didn't answer. The knock got harder and harder. She cracked the bathroom door to see where Neville was; he had fallen asleep. When she cracked open the door, the knocks got louder and he woke up. Precious shut the door back quietly. Neville stumbled to the door and asked, "Who is it?" "It's the manager, "There's a leak coming from this room; open the door." Neville said, "A leak?" and he cracked the door with the chain on it. When he did that, Precious heard a loud crash and a lot of fumbling in the room. She was afraid to open the door, and then she heard Malcolm's voice: "Precious, are you all right? Open the door; it's me, Malcolm." Precious was so happy to hear his voice; she opened the door crying and shaking. Malcolm just put his arms around her, and said, "It's all right now, it's all right." Precious just held on to him shaking and crying, saying "Thank you" repeatedly. Do you need a doctor, Precious?" Did he hurt you?" said Malcolm. "No," said Precious, "just my feelings."

Malcolm had come with Chauncey and two other guys; Neville was sitting on the floor bloody and naked. Chauncey picked up Precious's clothes and handed them to Malcolm. Malcolm gave Precious her clothes and told her to get dressed. Chauncey then came over to Malcolm, saying, "Is she all right, did he …?" "No," said Malcolm, "he didn't." Chauncey then went over to Neville and grabbed him by the throat; he told him, "This is a bad day for you, punk, get dressed." Neville got up and put on his clothes. Malcolm's two friends took Neville out somewhere.

When Precious came out of the bathroom, she said "Thank you" again to Malcolm and Chauncey, and she started to cry again, saying, "Please don't tell my sister." Malcolm looked at her and said, "Precious, this isn't something that we can keep a secret. I know I can't, and if Pretty ever finds out that I knew something happened to her baby sister, it won't be a good thing. Plus I'm on my way to meet her now." Precious then said, "I don't want to ruin the party tomorrow, Malcolm; please let's wait until after the dinner party and I promise I will tell my family. I feel so ashamed." "Don't feel shame, Precious, there are plenty of creeps like Neville who prey on young women. It's not your fault and some of them are real smooth," said Chauncey. "I felt something wasn't right with him, but I couldn't figure it out," said Precious. "Don't beat yourself up; it's a learning experience," said Chauncey.

Malcolm then said, "Precious, you have to promise me that you will tell your sisters or your parents or both, promise me." "I promise, Malcolm, but please, I want to wait until after the dinner party. I don't want to put a damper on things. Precious then said "Oh my God! I forgot, I was supposed to bring a date for the dinner party, Neville. What am I going to say when he doesn't come?" I don't want to ruin that night for anyone, Malcolm, what can I do?" She started crying again. Malcolm looked at Chauncey and Chauncey shook his head in a yes motion. Malcolm said, "I have an idea, Precious, stop crying." Malcolm then said, "Let's get out of here first. I'll explain on the way out."

When they got outside, Precious asked, "Where did your friends go, and where did Neville go?" "Don't worry about him, he'll be all right, but for sure he'll think twice before he tries to hurt someone else," said Chauncey. Malcolm then said, "Listen, Precious, we have an idea until after the dinner. Chauncey will be your dinner date that night; he's my good friend and he won't be out of place at dinner. All you have to do is tell your sisters and family that Chauncey is your date; Neville wasn't your type." "But they know I've been on the telephone with him all week." "How do they know it was him? Did they speak with him?" said Malcolm. "No they didn't." "Well, tell them it was Chauncey. They won't know the difference. Tell them you were talking to both of them but you decided on bringing Chauncey." "I don't know how to thank you both," she said, and she started crying again. Malcolm said, "Pull yourself together I have to go meet your sister and she is expecting you to come home and help." "I told her I went to check out a hotel with Neville; what would I say now?" "Tell her you checked it out and then you had to pick Chauncey up for me, now go have breakfast and pull yourself together. Chauncey will go with you." "I don't want to impose on Chauncey." "It's fine, Precious, actually it's my pleasure. Would you like me to drive? I know you are still a bit shaken," said Chauncey. Precious thanked him and handed him the keys.

Precious and Chauncey went out for breakfast and he was very understanding and sympathetic. Chauncey was quite comforting and a great listener. She explained what happened and her fainting and thinking it all was a dream. Chauncey stopped her from talking about it any more; he changed the subject and started talking about the upcoming wedding and the outfits they were wearing, because they both were in the wedding. After Chauncey had taken her mind off of what happened that morning, he told her he thought they should go now. Precious was much calmer and braver and ready to go.

She drove home with Chauncey and met up with Malcolm and Pretty. When she got in the house she broke the news to her family about Chauncey being her date for the dinner party, and how Neville wasn't her type. Panene looked relieved; she recognized something wasn't adding up but she left it alone. Pretty was so busy she didn't even pay much attention. The next day the dinner party went off without a hitch. Malcolm's family was down to earth and everyone had a wonderful time. Chauncey was concerned about Precious; she was on her third glass of wine, and she was starting to stare as if she was thinking too hard. He then asked her to walk to the car with him for a while; he felt she needed the break. She was very appreciative. Chauncey seemed to know exactly what she needed.

10. Precious's Confession and Pretty's Honeymoon
(Two Ps in a Pod)

It was a week after the engagement dinner party and Precious was doing everything she could to stay busy and away from her mom and dad. Malcolm's parents, Jennifer and Luther, were still in town. Pretty had the opportunity to work with Malcolm's mom, her mom, and her sister Princess on her wedding details. Precious was relieved that everyone was very busy and did not have the time to question her about anything or notice anything about her.

It was Sunday morning and Precious's telephone rang. It was Malcolm. He was very concerned about her, and about the fact that she had not told her family yet about her encounter with Neville. "Good morning," he said. "I'm just calling to check up on you and to find out when you are going to tell your folks." "I'm fine, Malcolm, they have been very busy this past week with your parents. I am going to tell them soon," she said. "Precious, I hope so," because I cannot keep it much longer and if you don't tell, I will, honey." "I know," Malcolm; I promise I'm going to tell them this week." "Do you want me to be there when you tell them?" he asked. "That may be a good idea," she said. "Thank you, I would let you know when." Malcolm than asked, "Have you heard anything from that creep?" "No, thank god, I haven't," said Precious. Then the two said good-bye and hung up.

When Malcolm hung up with Precious, he gave Chauncey a call. "What's up, man?" said Malcolm. "Everything is cool," said Chauncey. "What can I do for you this early in the morning, my brother?" "I just called Precious. I wanted to know when she was going to tell her folks," said Malcolm. Chauncey then said, "Yes, I wondered also. I didn't want to pressure her, and I know she's still feeling it". Malcolm said, "Yeah man, we have to encourage her to tell them, that's something you don't hide from your family. You need all the support you can get," "I agreed" said Chauncey, "but what can I do?" "Just bring it up when you talk with her or when you see her." Said Malcolm. "I will, man, I will, but I really don't want to put any pressure on her; she is very fragile right now," said Chauncey. "Hey man, you sound like you're getting attached or something," said Malcolm. "I'm concerned just like you are; that could have been my sister or mother," said Chauncey. "I know, but when you talk to her try to convince her. I'll talk with you later," said Malcolm.

Approximately one week later, Precious had gone to meet Malcolm and Chauncey for coffee; they wanted to speak with her together. When she arrived she started out by asking them to accompany her home to talk with her family. She knew that was the reason they both wanted to see her; both men were happy and definitely agreed to go with her. Precious was very nervous; however, she knew she had to tell them. She was smart enough to know that this was not something that you keep to yourself; it would not be healthy. Knowing that still did not stop her from feeling ashamed about the entire ordeal, or feeling that it was her fault for being so naïve.. In the short time that she knew him, she knew something wasn't right about him, and she ignored those feelings.

When the trio arrived at Precious's home, Pretty came to

the door. She was surprised to see Malcolm. She kissed him and they all came inside. Precious also knew that Princess would be there and it was the perfect night to talk with them all. Patrick, Panene, and Princess were in the den taking care of some business; Precious went in and asked if they had a moment, because she needed to speak with them. Patrick said, "Sure, honey, what is it?" Precious asked if they could come into the living room; Malcolm, Chauncey, and Pretty were in there already, and she wanted to speak with all of them. Penene looked puzzled; Patrick looked at his wife and said, "Oh boy, not another wedding so soon." Penene said, "Come on Patrick, stop speculating, please," and they entered the living room. Princess said, "Maybe she has a story for us," and chuckled.

Precious had everyone there and she was very nervous. Penene did not like the way her daughter looked and was thinking the worst, but did not know what. Pretty looked at her, then at Chauncey, and then at Malcolm, who would not look her in the eyes. Patrick just sat there quietly interested in what she had to say. Chauncey then got up and went over to Precious; he took her hand, as she was shaking, to give her some courage. Precious then began to tell her horrible story, about her encounter with Neville George.

Pretty sat with tears in her eyes holding on to Malcolm, silently thanking him for saving her sister. Princess cried and shouted, "Oh my God, you must have been sick keeping that to yourself all of this time, poor baby." Penene cried and hugged Precious like there was no tomorrow, apologizing to her for what happened. Patrick jumped up and said to Malcolm and Chauncey, "Where does this bastard live, I want to see him." Patrick was furious. Princess said, "We need to call the police." Malcolm and Chauncey just took Patrick to the side and were talking to him quietly without the women hearing. Pretty, Penene, and Princess kept reassuring Precious it was not her fault; he was just a creep. No one has the right to force himself or herself on a person, no one. Precious couldn't stop crying, but she felt a little relieved that it was out in the open. She now had the support of her family, and she did not realize how much she really needed that feeling. Patrick said, "No, we won't call the police." Then he walked over to his daughter and put his arms around her, silently crying with her, reassuring her, "It was not your fault, baby. Don't believe that it was; you trusted someone who was a creep. No man has the right to force himself on a woman, if he does, he's not a man. Baby, he's just no good, do you hear me?" Patrick then walked over to Malcolm and Chauncey shook their hands and hugged each one of them. "Thank you, from the bottom of my heart. That's my baby there," he said.

When the family stopped crying and reassuring Precious and making sure that she was all right, Pretty then said, "Well, what's up with you and Chauncey? Is it something or was it just because of this incident?" Chauncey looked over at Precious, and she managed to give him that innocent, sweet smile of hers and said, "I'm not really sure about anything right now; he's been a real friend through all of this." Malcolm just looked at his friend's face as Precious was talking. Chauncey didn't say a word; he just sat down and started talking to Malcolm about nothing. Penene then said, "Let's leave these young people alone for a while, honey." Princess said she had to leave; she was upset and had gotten a headache. Patrick then walked over to Malcolm, shook his hand again, and said, "I am very proud to have you join our family, very proud." He then looked at Chauncey, grabbed his hand, and said, "I don't know what to say yet, my brother," but looked over at Precious and winked his eye at Chauncey.

It was now the first week in February, the wedding was one week away. Neville George and the entire incident had finally become history. Precious was running around helping Pretty and Pretty was running herself crazy with the wedding, and driving poor Malcolm nuts in the process. The only thing on her mind was the honeymoon; she was still feeling a bit macho. Malcolm was just letting her enjoy herself; after all it was her wedding and weddings are for the bride. They weren't having a huge wedding, just a religious ceremony and a rather simple yet elegant reception. They were going to Aspen for their honeymoon, a winter wonderland, and a honeymoon suite in the most romantic hotel in Aspen. Malcolm was excited. Pretty didn't care where she went; she just wanted to go with him.

It was a day before the wedding and all the family was in town; they were spread out between the homes of Penene, Princess, and Malcolm. That night the sisters were together in Pretty's room, laughing and talking as they did before Princess's wedding. Pretty had a very small wedding party: Princess was her maid of honor and Precious was the maiden of honor. Malcolm had Chauncey as his best man and his cousin Steve as a groomsman. No flower girls or ring bearer. Both Malcolm and Pretty wanted something simple.

As the girls laughed and talked, Pretty reminded Princess how nervous she was the night before her wedding. Princess then asked Pretty why wasn't she nervous: "Maybe you did it already, that's why." Precious started laughing and said, "She has been trying to seduce that man every since the engagement." "Yes, that's true, but he is a wimp, he's scared," said Pretty. "I know one thing: he better be worth the wait or I'm going to seek an annulment the next day." "Girl, you are crazy; that man looks like he is going to put a hurting on you and keep your mouth shout for good," said Princess. Precious then said, "He shut her up when he first met her, she was so weak in the knees and speechless for once, you should have seen her, Princess. She broke out in a sweat, couldn't talk, she couldn't even breathe, so I know when he gets a hold of her, she might not survive." "Oh shut up, Precious, I can't wait until you get some, it will probably be Chaun ... cey." The three started laughing so loud that Penene came knocking on the door to see what was so funny. "Can I come in?" she said. Sure mom, come on in," said Pretty. "What's so funny?" Penene said. Princess told Penene what they were talking about, and Penene just laughed along with them. "I would love to be a fly on the wall," said Precious. "Me, too," said Princess, "because you know she won't tell us the truth when she comes back." "You will know when I come back, if I come back with a smile on my face, then you'll know he was all of that. If I come with papers in my hand, you know I got an annulment." "You are a fool," said Penene. "I don't know where you come from, I just don't know."

A few minutes later Patrick came and knocked on the door; he said he had a package for Pretty. "A package? Who could have sent me something tonight?" said Pretty. Patrick came in with two large boxes; Precious grabbed the card on the box and started to read it. "In a few hours you will be Mrs. Pretty Henry, I thought you could use this on our trip. I know for sure you'll look beautiful in it. Love, your husband in a few Malcolm." "Wow, that's nice, open it up, open it up!" shouted Penene. Pretty opened the first big box; it was a beautiful full-length brown mink coat with a hat to match. "Open the next box,: said Princess. Pretty grabbed the second box and opened it; it was a short fur jacket with matching boots, hat and gloves. Pretty said, "These gifts are beautiful but I don't plan to be outside much, unless I'm getting an annulment." Patrick said, "What?" "Don't ask," said Penene. "Let's go and leave these three alone." Patrick then said, "All I know is 'two down and one to go'" with a smile, and he and his wife left the girls alone.

The next day, the air was crisp and the sky was sunny, and everything went according to schedule. Pretty was a beautiful bride. She had on a straight white long-sleeve gown with a lace bodice and lace down the back and just enough down the sleeves, very elegant. Pretty took pride in her figure; she worked out regularly, so her dress fit her as if it was truly made for her. Her sisters were in deep violet dresses, with violet shoes. When they arrived at the ceremony, they had fur stoles draped around their shoulders. Pretty had a white fur stole draped around her. Once they came inside, aunt Shelly took the girls fur stoles, guess who was right there helping aunt Shelly with the stuff? Uncle Cadillac.

Everything that day went great and the reception was just

as great. Pretty couldn't wait to leave; Malcolm wanted to stay, he was having a good time. Pretty pulled him to the side and asked if they could leave now. Malcolm looked at her and smiled: "Sweetheart, we have a lifetime together. Don't rush, let us enjoy our family and friends." "Don't forget we have a flight to catch tonight," said Pretty. "Don't worry, we won't miss the flight. I promise."

After the reception, Pretty and Malcolm went to her house and changed their clothes for their flight. Chauncey and Malcolm's parents took all of their gifts to Malcolm's house, where they were going to live temporarily until they picked out a home. Malcolm had a two-bedroom condominium and his parents and cousins were staying there; they would be gone by the time Pretty and Malcolm returned from their honeymoon. Patrick was taking the two to the airport, and the luggage was already in the jeep. Pretty put on her full-length mink coat and they were off to the airport.

When they arrived in Aspen, the scenery was breathtaking, and the hotel picked them up in a limousine with complimentary champagne. The driver was congratulating them on their nuptials. Pretty was impressed.

When they arrived at the hotel, the honeymoon suite was something out of a magazine, with three rooms and a double bathroom. Each room had a fireplace. It was so beautiful. The living room had parquet floors, with large plush area rugs everywhere. In front of the fireplace was a uniquely made rug like a blanket made for two. The bedroom was carpeted with one huge fluffy area rug in front of a fireplace. The fire was roaring gently; it was warm and cozy in every room. The bedroom had mirrors all around the walls and on the ceiling; you could see the fire roaring everywhere. The effect was simply out of this world. In a medium-sized room connected to the bedroom was a large heart-shaped hot tub, which appeared to be lying on a large soft plush fluffy rug, so when you stepped out of the hot tub, your feet and/or your body would only touch this rug and it lead right back to the bedroom, with large heart-shaped mirrors all around. The layout was so romantic, and in every room there was a view of the snowy mountains and a bucket of champagne; it looked just like a postcard.

Pretty walked around the rooms impressed with everything, looking out of every window in amazement. Malcolm looked once, opened his suitcase, and went straight to the bathroom and got into the shower. He then called for his bride: "Where are you, Pretty, why aren't you in here with me?" When Malcolm called for her, it was the first time since she met him that she began to feel a bit nervous. This time she knew that Malcolm wasn't going to stop her, and she could not stop him. Tonight was the night. As she thought about tonight being the night, her stomach started to flood with rocks and needles, and she was stuck and did not know what to do. Malcolm called her again; this time she answered, "I'll get in when you get out." "No problem," he shouted back.

A few minutes later, while she was fumbling around in her suitcase, a vision of manliness came out of the bathroom. She had never seen Malcolm looking as radiant as he did this night, and he had on some wonderful-smelling cologne. He had a "groom" towel wrapped around his waist; he popped the cork on the champagne and poured two glasses and then laid in front of the fireplace. Malcolm's reflection was everywhere in the room. He looked over at his bride and told her to go shower and hurry back to her gay lover, and smiled. Pretty looked into Malcolm's eyes and her stomach tightened in a knot. Her body started ticking like a time bomb, every part ticking simultaneously. She knew this was real: tonight it would happen, and she slowly went trembling to the shower.

While she was in the shower she thought about how she was going to approach her new husband and how she was going to explore her options. As she showered she planned how she would mount her beauty and ride him into the sunset. The more she planned, the braver she became. Pretty had found a way to ward off her nervousness; all she had to do now was convince Malcolm of her plan. Pretty felt she was a smart and strong woman, and she knew she had been building Malcolm's desire for her. She had gotten a beautiful baby pink negligee for a shower gift and it fit her perfectly. She had a shape that would drive any man wild and she knew it, so her plot was to drive her husband insane, and she was now ready.

When she came out of the bathroom, Malcolm was sitting on the bed, still with the towel around his waist, sipping a glass of champagne. He spotted his bride in the many mirrors and he got up to greet her with a glass of champagne and a smile. "Mrs. Henry you look absolutely beautiful," he said and handed her the glass. Pretty smiled and took the glass. For an instant her heart started to tick faster, but she quickly calmed down, and she became the aggressor.

She sipped her champagne and then put her glass down. Pretty looked at her husband and said, "Mr. Henry, are you ready for this?" Malcolm gave her a huge smile and laughed a little. She then put her arms around his neck and started to kiss him slowly. Pretty glanced around at the window and snow was falling; it was beautiful. All you could see was white over huge mountains. She looked back around at Malcolm and slowly pushed him down on the bed, and she sat on him as if she was straddling a horse. Malcolm waited for her next move, appearing a bit shy. As Malcolm lay comfortably as his wife played on top of him, teasing and caressing him, he just let her enjoy herself. Pretty was feeling very bold and in complete control.

As the fireplace roared and crackled, Malcolm decided it was time to show his wife who was in charge of this sleigh ride. He was in his playing field, and she really knew nothing about this ride. Her bold attitude and thirst for the ride was what gave her the courage to pretend. Plus she was very naïve to believe that her experienced husband was that shy.

As Pretty felt she was doing something caressing and preparing for the ride, Malcolm decided to come alive. When he came alive, Pretty started to tremble in fear. She had never seen a sleigh so firm and straight as Malcolm's; hell, she had never seen one that she would ever ride anyway. Malcolm began to slowly and gently lead his bride to the bottom of the tallest mountain that she had ever imagined, and cautiously drag her and his sleigh up to the top of that mount. With each passionate step that he took, Pretty sighed and screamed with fright, a fear that had entered her body like an avalanche, building up for a great tumble, and she knew with each climb up that snowy mountain she had to come down on this same sleigh. Pretty's bravery quickly disappeared, and she knew that Malcolm was in full control of everything, and for the first time in her life she was sincerely terrified and didn't know if she would make it down alive. She screamed out to Malcolm, "No baby, I can't, I can't, I can't." As she screamed out to him, she happened to look up and there she saw their reflection a hundred times in the mirrors all around and that is when Pretty left this planet.

That's when Malcolm took his bride for the ride of her life. When she reached the top of that wonderful mountain, there he took his Pretty on a scenic route, and she went up and down and around the entire mountain, not missing a sight. Pretty held on and screamed all the way; Malcolm knew it wasn't a scream of pain but one of complete ecstasy. As Malcolm drove and steered his sleigh down that mount, Pretty's avalanche was growing rapidly and massively, as her husband brought her swiftly, yet passionately down that mountain. When they both reached the bottom together, the sleigh and the avalanche, Pretty trembled as if the mountain had a volcano in the middle of winter that had just erupted. At that very moment there was a huge explosion, and the lava spurted out hot and thick, and as Pretty lay smothered, she shook in disbelief at the entire ride and thought, *It's over, it's over.* Suddenly, Malcolm switched positions with his wife and had her take the sleigh up for a ride. Pretty fought and shouted, "We can't, not again, not yet baby, not yet!" Malcolm grabbed her arms firmly but gently, pulled her close to him, and held her tight in his arms, saying, "It's all right, honey, I'll wait, but I know you can handle it, Pretty, I know you can."

Pretty jumped off the sleigh, went straight to the fireplace, and laid on her belly, sobbing in ecstasy, shaking like she had never shaken before, in disbelief. She couldn't believe the feeling she was experiencing. Suddenly, she felt her husband softly touch her back and cover her with the fuzzy cover in front of the fireplace. "Sweetheart, are you all right? Did I hurt you in any way? How do you feel?" Pretty could not talk; she just shook her head no, and then she turned around with her eyes closed and hugged Malcolm tight and cried. As she cried she trembled, and he felt her heart beat, and her shapely body was as hot as the fire in front of them. The heat from Pretty's body stimulated Malcolm, and he lifted Pretty up into his arms and carried her to the next room to the heart-shaped Jacuzzi. Pretty was at his mercy; he carried her in. As they entered, Malcolm wrapped his legs around her waist as he kissed every bit of exposed flesh. Pretty did not know what to do next, but Malcolm did everything. He caressed her until the heat in the tub and the heat in her body began to boil; at that moment, Malcolm lifted her again, laid her on the fluffy carpet, and caressed her every curve. As her avalanche grew again, Malcolm stopped it from rolling and he slowly melted it with his tongue. As he introduced his melter to his wife, she started crying out, "Oh God, Malcolm, Oh God, Malcolm, I'm sorry baby, I'm sorry." As the melter slowly met every inch of that beautiful avalanche and successfully melted it, as the water flowed onto Malcolm he too melted, and the two just melted together and merged like marshmallows in hot chocolate, and all you could hear was the crackling fireplaces and sweet moans from his bride. Malcolm was now in control, and Pretty knew it.

As Malcolm looked at his bride, he thought to himself; *Life does not always go according to plans; some of us made mistakes before marriage. However, you don't have to keep repeating the mistake. When you meet someone that you think is special, save yourself for that person. Having sex or making love right away can block your true feelings, and lust will block it every time. Learn to love them first for who they are and if they are for you they will respect the wait. Love will come and be more meaningful and lasting, with no regrets.* Malcolm then whispered in his bride's ear, "Aren't you glad you waited for me?"

Sex is something that will have you searching for better
But love is something that will last forever
Which will you choose?

About the Author

E. K. Cooper was born in the mid-1950s in the heart of the Bedford-Stuyvesant community of Brooklyn, New York. She was raised in a very strict Barbadian home where G-d, education, morals, and respect were promoted consistently.

She was married twice and is presently widowed. She has four successful sons, three daughters-in-law, three grandsons, and two granddaughters. E.K's family is the joy and center of her life.

E.K.'s focus was placed on keeping her four sons from becoming negative statistics in society. Her greatest accomplishment in life has been rearing her children to fear and love G-d, and completing this book. Her focus now is helping in the socialization and rearing of her grandchildren in hopes to inspire them to set high standards and maintain values as they grow and mature.

She has spent many years volunteering and teaching young children in various religious settings while working two, sometimes three jobs. E.K. is very proud that she mentors young girls, being able to lend an ear as they mature into womanhood.

The issue of teen pregnancy and unwed parents has inspired her to prayerfully give young men and women information regarding securing and possibly setting high values and goals for themselves.

E.K. was asked what she wishes to accomplish from her book;

she answered: "I hope that the stories will be relevant to the lives of the readers, and that they may envision themselves in the body of my work. If that can happen, then my expectations for this book will be accomplished.

E.K. was asked about her future plans and possible retirement. She answered: "I picture myself on Accra beach in Christ Church, Barbados, satisfied that I made a difference in some young person's life. Knowing that and being able to take a dip in the sea would be enough for me."

Remember
Start out to inspire many
And help a few
Make a difference in one
And you'll be inspired too

By E. K. Cooper
2/27/09